What the critics are saying

"FORBIDDEN, the first adventure of the SERAPHINE CHRONICLES, is magical, light, and relentlessly erotic."
- *Ann Leveille, Sensual Romance*

"Cheyenne McCray has done an impressive job creating a lusty romance that titillates your imagination, sets your senses free and keeps you flipping the pages from sheer excitement."
- *Jan Springer, Romance Author for The Road to Romance*

"FORBIDDEN was just the type of book to keep you turning pages. There are plenty of suspenseful elements here to keep your attention. The sensuality of this book is incredibly hot."
- *Robin Taylor, In The Library Review*

D0064334

Discover for yourself why readers can't get enough of the multiple-award-winning publisher Ellora's Cave. Whether you prefer e-books or paperbacks, be sure to visit EC on the web at www.ellorascave.com for an erotic reading experience that will leave you breathless.

www.ellorascave.com

Ellora's Cave Publishing, Inc.
PO Box 787
Hudson, OH 44236-0787

ISBN # 1-84360-560-0

Seraphine Chronicles Book 1: Forbidden, 2002.

Seraphine Chronicles Book 1: Forbidden edited by Ann Richardson.
Cover art by Darrell King.

Warning: The following material contains strong sexual content meant for mature readers. SERAPHINE CHRONICLES BOOK 1: FORBIDDEN has been rated NC-17, erotic, by a minimum of three independent reviewers. We strongly suggest storing this book in a place where young readers not meant to view it are unlikely to happen upon it. That said, enjoy…

SERAPHINE CHRONICLES BOOK 1: FORBIDDEN

Written by

CHEYENNE MCCRAY

To F.A.F:

My own private fantasy man.

Acknowledgment:

Many thanks to Annie Windsor
Without you, my rhyme would have no reason

Chapter One

Tanzinite woman, wingless and wan

Nordai of Power, of twins, we warn

One path to doom, enslavement and walls

With unholy mating, Dair rises or falls

Chronicles of the Seraphine Elves...XXVII

Candlelight flickered across Liana's skin as the last of her clothing pooled at her feet. The scent of jensai blooms floated through the open window on an evening breeze, the balmy air easing over her body like a lover's caress.

Liana stood in the center of her bedchamber and closed her eyes, a vision of the dark stranger filling her senses. As she tilted her head back, her hair brushed her bare buttocks like a whisper of moonlight.

Like she imagined the man's touch would be upon her skin.

Even as she moved her hands to her naked breasts, she was aware of the nordai's passionate night calls outside her cottage. But the raven's cries faded as the stranger's image burned in Liana's thoughts.

Black eyes that had followed her as she had made her way through the tavern. Sensuality simmering beneath the surface of his stare. Ebony hair brushing his broad shoulders. A scruffy hint of a beard along his arrogant jaw. Muscles that flexed with every movement as he towered over her.

Visualizing the stranger's calloused hands upon her body, Liana caressed her taut nipples with her palms. She could almost smell the man's woodsy scent, a hint of which she had caught when she had brushed past him in the tavern. She had shivered from the slight contact, but kept her gaze averted, every nerve ending ablaze with wanting him.

How could she desire a man she had never seen before today?

How could she desire any man when it was *forbidden*?

A moan eased through Liana's lips as the vision of the stranger's touch grew stronger. She imagined his tanned fingers covering her pale breast, his calloused palm chaffing her sensitive nipples. She could feel the black hair on his powerful arms brushing her skin. Her body ached with desire, ached with need. A need she did not understand how to fill.

There was only one being with whom she was supposed to mate—but no. She would not allow that reality to spoil the erotic fantasy weaving through her mind.

She had never mated with a man, for it was forbidden. She had heard lusty tales told by her heart-sister Tierra and the tavern wenches, but Liana had never had such an intense desire to experience such a joining—

Until *him*.

Her belly quivered as she eased one hand down her flat stomach to the tangle of curls between her thighs. Where it was forbidden to touch herself. The place that now ached to be stroked, as though that might ease her wanting of the stranger.

Liana's tresses moved as an extension of her thoughts, sliding over her naked skin like she imagined the stranger might touch her body. His hands would be slow. Gentle. His mouth would feel hot on her lips, her breasts, her belly, leaving a trail of fire wherever he touched.

Burning.

Slipping her fingers between her folds, Liana gasped as she felt the dampness of her desire for the dark stranger. Her other hand continued to knead her nipples as she imagined the man fondling them. Her hair caressed her shoulders down to her hips, and the motion of her fingers grew stronger, more insistent, as she stroked her clit.

But instead of relieving her need for the man, the knot in her belly grew tighter and tighter yet.

She could almost feel the stranger's stubble, rough against her inner thighs. And his tongue — gods, his tongue — laving at her clit that was building with pressure. Building and building and —

A cry of surprise rose in Liana's throat and her eyes flew open as the most exquisite sensations rocked through her. Like a flock of startled blackbirds bursting from their roosts amongst the sacred vines. Like moonlight sparkling across the rainbow sands of Mairi.

Her fingers continued, drawing out the intense feelings until her body could take no more.

Liana dropped to her knees and braced her palms against the rush-covered floor, her hair swinging forward to cover her face. Her breasts swayed and her thighs trembled. Her breath came in short gasps as she struggled to overcome the dizziness that threatened to render her boneless.

When she had strength to move, Liana eased onto her haunches. A sound, ever so slight, pierced the haze still shrouding her confused mind. Through her curtain of hair, she glanced up to see an enormous ebony nordai perched on her windowsill, its black eyes focused intently on her — and a sheath was strapped to its powerful leg. The hilt of a dagger jutted out, a ruby glinting on its hilt like a drop of blood.

Ice chilled Liana's spine. *My gods — what have I done?*

* * * * *

Aric sucked in his breath as the Tanzinite maid collapsed to the floor with the strength of her orgasm. He had known he was breaching Liana's privacy when she had begun to shed her clothing — but he had been too enchanted to move.

And Lord Ir, when she had touched herself, he had nearly come undone. The flushed look of utter surprise and rapture on Liana's face when she had climaxed had been the most beautiful sight he had ever seen.

It had been all he could do to maintain his nordai form. Gods, how he had wanted to fly through her open window, resume his man's body and bury his cock inside her slit, claiming her virgin warmth and fucking her until she screamed her pleasure. How he wanted to be the cause of the ecstasy in those sea green eyes.

Forbidden.

She was of the Tanzinites, the cave-dwellers, and he of the Nordain, the Sky People. Never had the two races mated. Never would they.

Forbidden.

This was the woman who had been named to mate with the Sorcerer Zanden, a Nordain traitor. It was a joining Aric was sworn to prevent—by whatever means deemed necessary.

Forbidden.

The maid sat back upon her haunches, her breasts rising and falling with every breath, her flaxen hair shrouding her delicate features. She was a rare Tanzinite, born without wings, banished from the caves at birth and forced to live on Dair's surface amongst humans and fey folk.

Yet she was perfection. Candlelight danced across her silken skin, as beautiful as a Mairi pearl. Her nipples were the deep rose of the sacred vine's blossoms. The pale curls between her thighs like sea foam. And her hair, moonbeams spilling in shimmering waves past her hips.

His keen senses caught her scent as it rose up to him through the open window. Liana smelled of jensai blooms and moonlight. And of the passion between her thighs, a nectar of which he desired to drink his fill.

A lustful sound escaped Aric—and the maid's attention riveted on him. Even through her fine hair, he saw her sea green eyes widen with shock and fear. For a long moment their gazes remained locked, until Aric forced himself to move.

With a mighty flap of his wings, he took to the dark skies, trying to shove the erotic memories of the Tanzinite woman from his mind. He had a task to complete, and that did *not* include joining with the maid.

Though how in Lord Ir's name he would keep his hands off Liana, he did not know.

* * * * *

Shivering, more from the memory of what she had done last night than from this eve's chill, Liana drew her cloak tighter. She hurried as she made her way through Fiorn, a village in Sorcerer Zanden's realm.

Uba, a cruel and vicious woman, had raised Liana, along with two other orphaned girls — Ranelle and Tierra. Long ago Uba would have sold each of them into prostitution if it had not been for payments made to the greedy woman by an unknown benefactor. Uba had died only weeks ago, leaving the three young women the small cottage they had grown up in.

Now that it was dark, by Zanden's orders, Liana was allowed to leave her home to perform her Seer's duties. From the time she was old enough to communicate, Liana had seen visions of the future, and occasionally of the past. Early on, Uba had taken advantage of Liana's skills, arranging for Liana to tell fortunes for *ansi* stones. Of course, Uba had snatched all payments from Liana. It was a wonder Liana had managed to hoard away a few *ansi* that Uba had been unaware of.

Unlike Liana, Ranelle's and Tierra's magical powers were unknown to anyone outside the three of them, so they had never been exploited in the same manner. Instead, Ranelle had been forced to perform a nightly erotic dance, and Tierra usually tended the bar.

As she hurried toward the tavern, Liana's cloak and thin gown brushed over cobblestones, the material making only a whisper of sound. She knew her way by rote and by her senses, not requiring the moonlight to see by. Normally Liana walked with her friends from the cottage to the tavern. However, on this day, Tierra was ill from a bout with food poisoning, and Ranelle had gone to the cobbler's.

Liana's thoughts turned back to last eve, when she had been alone in her bedchamber — or thought she had been. Gods, how could she have been so foolish? The nordai at her windowsill hadn't been one of the ravens that thrived on Dair. It had been much too large — and the sheath and dagger strapped to its powerful leg told her it was no common nordai. The raven had been one of the Nordain, the Sky People who transformed from raven form to human at will, and usually dwelled in a kingdom far to the north.

But if the being was one of Zanden's minions, one of the Nordain traitors who had pledged allegiance to the Sorcerer, her life might be forfeit.

But then her life may as well be over if she was forced to join with him.

No!

Pausing at the center of a quiet alleyway, Liana gritted her teeth and struggled to maintain her composure. She pressed her hand against the *ansi* gems sewn within her cloak, and reaffirmed the decision she had made earlier. It was time to make her escape. She would not wait until moonchange, when Zanden would be relegated to his nordai form and forced to remain at his fortress along with his Nordain minions.

Tonight.

She would go tonight.

Cool air carried the scent of the Mairi Sea, blending with the strong perfume of jensai blooms that surrounded Fiorn. Liana tried to ignore the less attractive odors of dung and garbage strewn beside the village's business establishments, but it was near impossible.

No, she wouldn't miss this place where she had been forced to live since her birth.

Since her own people abandoned her. Discarded her for her differences.

Even though she had known of it since her childhood, until of late, it hadn't seemed real—that Zanden had chosen her as his mate. That he would come for her after moonchange, shortly before she reached her twentieth season. That he believed she was the Tanzinite maid and he the Nordain male of the prophecy.

The prophecy the Elves made before her birth.

If she had not seen it in her own visions, likely she would never have believed it to be true.

Revulsion flooded Liana in an icy wave and she shivered despite her cloak. She had never seen the Sorcerer beyond a vision or two, yet she couldn't bear the thought of his hands upon her body. His stave impaling her, driving into her, planting his wicked seed within her womb. All to fulfill the prophecy and ensure his rule over every race.

She knew only too well how the Sorcerer dealt with treachery amongst his servants. Uba had said that Zanden insisted Liana would experience fornication by his hands and body alone. If the Sorcerer learned she had done the forbidden after he had decreed to all of Dair that he owned her…if he learned she had touched herself and brought such pleasure to her own body…

Liana shuddered. Her head could soon hang from the walls of the Sorcerer's fortress for her disobedience. Her sightless eyes would stare out at the Mairi Sea alongside countless others who had failed or betrayed Zanden.

The hood of her cloak fell to her shoulders as she glanced to the dark sky. Zanden needed her to fulfill the prophecy. He would be more likely to chain her naked to his dungeon wall as punishment, forcing himself upon her whenever he wished.

No, no, no! She would *never* mate with any Nordain man of power, as the prophecy had foretold. Along with Ranelle and Tierra, Liana would escape and vanish forever from the Sorcerer's realm. Far from his reach. And far from the ranges of any Nordain flyer.

Raising her chin, she blocked the horrible image of the Sorcerer from her mind and once again started toward the tavern. But another, far more powerful vision replaced thoughts of the Sorcerer, and she stopped in mid-stride.

The stranger.

No matter the future Liana would face if she did not escape soon, she couldn't rid her thoughts of the devastating man from the tavern. The way that smoky black gaze had studied her every movement last eve. Raw masculinity that called to her woman's core. The hard line of his jaw every time a man approached her to have his fortune told.

As though the stranger was *jealous*.

Dampness seeped between Liana's thighs and her nipples puckered against the light material of her gown at the mere thought of the man desiring her body. After feeling such incredible pleasure at her own hands, she could imagine the dark stranger taking her to far greater heights. Of its own mind, her hair moved within her cloak, sliding across her breasts, enhancing the need that grew tighter and tighter within her belly.

Ye gods! Liana stamped her foot and clenched her fists, and her tresses went still. As she tucked her hair behind her pointed ear, she tried to calm her desires. She had no time for the newly awakened fantasies.

Tonight she must make her escape. But first she had to convince—

"You had best hurry along now, wench."

Liana startled at the sound of Ranelle's voice from behind her. Hand to her pounding heart, Liana whirled to confront her friend. "You nearly caused my lifeforce to depart!"

Ranelle tossed her long mahogany hair over her shoulder as she gave an impish grin, her teeth flashing in the moonlight. "That should teach you to fantasize in the middle of the village about handsome strangers."

Heat flushed through Liana, and she was certain she was as red as a jensai bloom. "I was doing no such—"

"Save untruths for someone who might believe them." Ranelle brushed away Liana's protest with a wave of her hand, the motion causing her cloak to gape open, revealing sparkling attire, generous curves and dark nipples jutting under the sheer material of her gown.

"Wh-what are you talking about?" Liana muttered, but at the same time she wondered if her friend had ever touched her own nipples, or caressed herself between her thighs as Liana had done.

"Last night Tierra and I noticed how you stumbled through your dealings with the patrons." Ranelle laughed and in sisterly fashion adjusted Liana's hood so that it once again covered her pale tresses. "And how you could not keep your eyes off the big brute in the corner who watched you the entire eve."

"You have a fine imagination." Cheeks burning ever hotter, Liana ducked her head and started toward the tavern again. "Come, lest Nira send her guard after us."

"Ah, but you forget." Ranelle easily kept up, her long legs outpacing Liana's shorter ones. "I, too, am gifted with sight."

Liana stopped, forcing Ranelle to back up a few paces. Her breath caught as she whispered, "What did you see?"

Ranelle cast her gaze over her shoulder as if looking for someone in the darkness. When she turned back to Liana, she offered a half-smile. "Only that this man is a part of your future."

Swallowing past the lump in her throat, Liana fisted her hands in the folds of her cloak, drawing it tighter yet. "In what way?"

"I do not know." Ranelle shrugged but looked uneasy as she drew the opening of her own cloak closed, covering her near-naked breasts. "Even though the brute did naught but scowl whenever his glance fell upon me, my senses tell me he is one *you* can trust."

"Trust." The word slipped from Liana's lips, a mocking sound even to her own ears. "As if I can trust any soul on the whole of this world."

At the hurt expression on Ranelle's lovely face, Liana hurried to add, "Except you and Tierra, of course. Only the two of you."

Ranelle winked, her eyes shimmering silver in the moonlight. "*Halia*. As if I would question your trust in me. As you would never question my trust in you or Tierra."

"You are both my heart-sisters, truth." Liana hugged Ranelle tight. As always, her friend smelled of exotic spices and vanilla.

A wolf's howl echoed through the night, and Liana shivered. *Come with me*, she said in Ranelle's mind. *Tonight*.

"It is not safe!" Ranelle's voice rose a fraction above a whisper and her glance darted around the darkened village, as though concerned they were being followed. She leaned forward to murmur in Liana's ear, "We agreed to escape with Tierra during moonchange. And besides, our heart-sister is still ill. She would not be able to accompany us."

Liana sighed and urged her friend toward their destination, wishing Ranelle could speak in thought to ensure they wouldn't be overheard. They were within feet of the weathered building where they were both forced to work each night. Crude laughter and voices came from inside the establishment. Stinking odors of sour ale and vomit outside the tavern's door churned her stomach.

I — we must all go now, she told Ranelle.

"A vision?"

Liana glanced up to see Ranelle's frown, knowing her friend would expect an explanation. An explanation Liana was too embarrassed to give without working up her courage. How could she tell her friend how she had touched herself intimately — and that a Nordain had watched her?

No, not a vision...more a feeling, Liana finally replied.

"A *feeling*?" Ranelle's jaw dropped, a look of protest on her face.

Liana's tresses vibrated and ice prickled her skin. She held up her hand to stop the rant she knew was forthcoming from her friend.

Something is watching us, Halia. Pressure pounded Liana's temples as she forced the thought to Ranelle. *We best get inside. Now!*

* * * * *

Aric ruffled his feathers and turned his gaze from the Tanzinite maid and the *gishla*. His grasp tightened on his perch upon the tavern's roof as his eyes hunted the night sky for irani.

Only black sky and pale stars.

But his senses told him the Sorcerer's winged beasts were close. Much too close.

It isn't time.

Zanden must have learned of the plans to steal the Tanzinite maid from beneath the Sorcerer's very nose.

Which would certainly mean another traitor existed in the midst of Aric's court.

Or the bastard simply knows too well how I think.

Aric spread his massive wings and soared from the tavern's roof, his gaze searching the village to ensure his change would not be witnessed. Even as his claws touched the ground, he transformed into his Nordain human form. His feathers melded into the tunic, breeches and boots he needed to clothe himself. The sheathed dagger that had been strapped to his leg now rested at his hip, and the gem at its hilt glowed like a single red eye.

Lord Ir. If Jalen, Aric's Elvin brother-at-arms, did not arrive soon, all might be for naught. *What could be keeping him?*

As Aric put his hand to the tavern door, he paused to whistle for Baethel. The stallion's answering whinny came from behind the building, along with the wolf Toen's soft growl. Aric whistled again, telling his companions of the change in plans. They would not wait until the tavern closed this eve.

He would take her now.

Aric's cock hardened at the double meaning of his thought, and he gritted his teeth. He had no business thinking such. His duty was to his people and to keep the prophecy from fulfillment.

He shoved the tavern door open, smoke from the hearth, sour ale and filth clouding his senses. Pausing a moment, he sought to catalogue each and every patron within the establishment before he moved forward and pushed his way through the crowd.

The tavern was packed with men stuffing their guts with ale and meat, and feasting their eyes upon the tavern wenches, Liana and the *gishla*. Aric narrowed his gaze as he saw the brunette *gishla* nearly naked and dancing on a platform at the center of the room. Her large breasts swayed as she moved. Her dark nipples and the mound between her thighs were easily seen through the transparent material of her scrap of a dress.

She was beautiful, yes, but he had the strong desire to yank the wench from the platform, wrap her in a dozen blankets and send her far from this hideous place. For some odd reason her near nakedness caused a knot to form in his gut.

His scowl moved from the *gishla* to the crowd of leering men. He would like to rip the eyes from every man staring at the maid. Cheers rose around Aric as the *gishla* performed her erotic dance, and it was all he could do to control himself.

What ailed him so?

He forced his attention from the *gishla* to the corner of the tavern, where Liana stood as she told fortunes to one bastard after another. She had her palm to a man's sweaty forehead, her eyes closed, her lips moving. Aric's keen hearing caught the words she spoke, but they were of no import — a simple fortune for the simple man before her.

Aric shoved his way through the crowd, attempting to ignore a yellow-haired wench who rubbed her full breasts against him, her hardened nipples sliding across his bicep as he moved past.

"Suck yer cock fer one *ansi*, love," the wench crooned. "Spread me legs and fuck ye fer two." She latched onto his arm and he caught the sour smell of ale on her breath as she pressed close. "Aye, fer you, I would fuck all night."

With little difficulty he shrugged off the woman, leaving her to ply her wares with some other fool.

When Aric was mere feet from the Tanzinite maid, he paused to watch. Liana was petite, dwarfed by those who surrounded her, yet she stood straight, her shoulders back, as though she feared no man. She was obviously deep in trance, oblivious to the bastards who ogled her body as she told the man his fortune.

Aric's jaw tightened and he clenched his fists as fury built within him, like lava rising within Mount Taka. He would like naught more than to lay waste every bastard leering at Liana.

A sheer garment draped her small form, similar to what the *gishla* wore. Liana may as well have been completely naked for all the good it did. The only thing protecting her from being ravaged by the heathens around her was the Sorcerer's claim on her. Threat enough that no man would dare lay a finger on the Tanzinite maid.

As Aric studied Liana, the noisy din of the tavern faded until all he could hear was her musical voice telling the man his fortune. He caught her scent of jensai blooms and moonlight that was somehow untainted by the smoke and ale stench of the tavern. She was so lovely, even more so than even the sensual Elvin women, for whom so many ballads of love were written.

For days he had watched Liana, preparing for the time he would take her. He had enjoyed watching her — the way she moved, her quick smile for her friends, and her kindness to those around her. Liana was beauty and grace, like a rose among thorns.

He swallowed, hard, as the image of Liana, naked in her bedchamber, filled his mind. Pebble-hard nipples, pert breasts, and hair the color of moonbeams caressing her rounded buttocks. Her fingers sliding into her slit, the smell of her sex. The look of ecstasy upon her face, and her sweet cry as she climaxed.

His rigid cock ached with the need to bury himself inside her core. He visualized her smiling at him, her sea green eyes beckoning. Her soft voice telling him to come to her as she lay on her back, her thighs spread, and her nipples swollen from his mouth and hands. She would beg him to thrust his cock inside her. He would fuck her again and again —

Liana's eyes snapped open and she snatched her hand from the man's forehead. She stumbled back against the tavern wall as her attention cut from the man to Aric. Her lips parted as her gaze locked with his.

Blood rushed in his ears as the moment stretched between them. Her heart pounded loud enough for his sensitive hearing to discern, its rhythm matching his own. She pressed her hand between her breasts, as if to slow her ragged breathing, and her nipples peaked beneath her sheer clothing.

And then the knowledge came to Aric as clear as if Liana had spoken.

She wanted him as much as he wanted her.

Lord Ir.

Aric opened and closed his fists and hardened his jaw.

No. He could not take the chance of being near Liana. He desired her too much, and he knew with certainty that she would welcome him into her body.

Jalen would have to take responsibility for the Tanzinite maid.

Aric pivoted on his heel. It took everything he had to walk away from Liana.

Chapter Two

Liana's face burned as she watched the stranger force his way back through the crowded tavern and toward the door. The man was so tall she could see his raven head above all others.

Even as he strode away, her heart continued to pound against her palm. She pressed her hand tighter to her chest, struggling to control her churning emotions. And she tried in vain to suppress the images that had burst into her mind, interrupting her trance.

Images of the stranger naked and between her thighs, their sweat-slick skin sliding together. Him, thrusting his hard cock into her quim and fucking her repeatedly as she screamed in ecstasy and begged for more. She had *felt* his calloused palms clenching her hips, his mouth on her nipples, his hot muscled body pressed against hers.

A hand clasped Liana's wrist, jerking her attention back to the smoky tavern. She shivered and blinked, and looked up into Nira's frigid blue eyes.

The barkeeper scowled. "Ye best be gettin' back ta work, wench."

Liana glanced to the rough hand gripping her wrist and narrowed her eyes as her gaze returned to the foul woman. "Release me," Liana commanded.

Nira's jaw dropped. "Dare ye—"

A trance slammed into Liana hard and fast. Reflexively, her free hand shot up and she pressed her palm to Nira's sweaty forehead.

Everything around Liana vanished as her lids fluttered shut.

No sight. No sound.

And then a vision burst into her mind.

They are coming.

The Sorcerer's winged beasts and his Nordain minions.

The tavern – on fire. Men shouting. Women screaming.

I – I cannot breathe. Smoke fills my lungs. Fire licks at my clothing.

A man. Grabs me from behind. He's taking me –

"*No!*" The scream pierced the tavern's clamor, and Liana's eyelids flew open. Her body turned to ice as she realized the scream had come from her own throat.

Nira dropped Liana's wrist and staggered back, her blue eyes wide with terror. "Witch! Get outta me tavern afore I throw ye out."

Liana's tresses vibrated as she stared at the sea of faces gaping at her in the now silent room.

"It is too late," she whispered.

* * * * *

At the same moment Aric heard Liana's scream from inside the tavern, he caught the sound of flapping wings. Powerful wings, bearing down on the village of Fiorn.

The irani. Coming to take Liana to the Sorcerer!

"Gods, *damn*," Aric shouted as his gaze raked the sky. *Where is Jalen? And what of Renn?*

But it was not his brother Renn flying toward him. It was the irani. At least a dozen of the massive beasts.

Fury pounding in his temples, Aric cursed again and plunged back into the tavern. Even as he shoved his way through the crowd, the beasts' eerie shrieks rent the air.

"The Sorcerer's devils!" shouted a woman. "They be coming for us!"

Pandemonium exploded throughout the tavern. Men yelled. Women screamed. Tables and chairs crashed to the floor.

Hot bodies thrust past Aric, impeding his progress. It took all the strength he had to keep from being swept with the crowd back toward the door. He had to get to Liana. Had to spirit her away before the irani found her.

He heard thumps on the tavern roof and knew at least half a dozen of the irani had landed on the thatch. Aric had only moments before the beasts would be inside.

A bar wench jumped from a tabletop, in her haste knocking over a lantern with her hip. Flames shot across the rush and ale covered floor. Smoke gripped Aric's lungs and blurred his vision. He saw the *gishla* being grabbed from her dancing table, and then the brunette vanished into the mob.

Aric resisted the impulse to help the *gishla.* His eyes watered from the smoke as he searched for Liana. *There.* Over the crowd he could just make out her small form. She had a stool in her hands and was swinging it at a windowpane. At the same time she screamed, "Ranelle! Over here!"

As the glass shattered, more irani shrieks echoed throughout the village. More pounding on the tavern roof.

Smoke and fire engulfed the room. Timbers splintered and cracked as the irani ripped into the thatch above.

Aric stumbled over a body, the poor soul trampled from the stampede of people. He did not dare stop. He had to reach Liana.

He was within feet of her as she swung the stool at the window again, breaking away more of the glass. She reached toward the opening at the same moment an irani thrust its hideous head through, its jaws wide.

Aric ripped his dagger from its sheath. Liana screamed as the irani clamped its beak around her wrist.

The irani yanked Liana forward, dragging her half through the window. Smoke burned Aric's eyes as he lunged forward and clasped Liana around her waist. At the same moment, Aric sliced the jagged edge of his dagger through the irani's thin neck, severing the beast's head from its body.

Liana screamed and fought against Aric's hold, obviously out of her mind with terror. Heat from the fire burned at his nape as he struggled to force the Tanzinite maid through the window. He coughed, near overcome from smoke as he shoved her over the sill, while at the same time trying not to tear her delicate skin on the remaining shards of glass.

She cried out as she tumbled through the window and landed on the dead irani. Aric started out through the opening, whistling for Toen and Baethel as he climbed. Glass scraped his skin as he forced his huge frame through the window and then jumped to the ground.

Liana scrambled to her feet, moonlight illuminating her face and sheer clothing. Even as smoke billowed from the window, she attempted to force her way past Aric, trying to get back into the tavern.

"Are you daft, wench?" Aric grasped her around the waist. She kicked and screamed as he threw her over his shoulder. "You'll get yourself killed!"

"Ranelle!" Liana shouted. "I must help Ranelle!"

The sound of pounding hooves alerted Aric to Baethel's approach. The stallion rounded the corner of the burning tavern, galloping straight toward Aric and Liana. Toen howled as he loped at the horse's heels.

"If your friend is still in the tavern," Aric said as he lifted Liana to toss her onto Baethel's back. "She's as good as dead now."

"No!" Liana shouted, her heart leaping into her throat. "Let me help her, you—you son of an irani!"

Coarse hair chafed Liana's skin as the man ignored her cries and flung her across a horse's withers. Her thin gown hiked up to her waist, exposing her bare bottom, and she screamed with rage as she fought to free herself.

The stranger easily pinned both her wrists to her backside with one hand as he mounted the horse. No matter how hard she fought him, she could not free her arms from her captor. Before she knew it, he had tied her wrists together with a strap, just above her naked hips.

When she again shouted at him to let her go, the stranger slid a piece of cloth into her mouth and tied it behind her head, gagging her. Liana went limp, realizing it was useless to fight. She knew had to conserve her strength and use her wiles to escape.

And escape she would.

"Toen, search for Jalen and Renn," the man commanded. From her upside down position, Liana could barely make out the form of a white wolf as the beast howled and then trotted into the crowd of screaming villagers. Heat from the fire warmed her skin and she could barely breathe from the smoke.

The stranger kept Liana face down, her belly across his lap, her hands still tied behind her back. Her hair fell forward, covering her face, and her gown hiked even farther, almost up to her breasts. "To the Elves' pool, Baethel," the man growled.

The horse bolted into the night, jolting Liana and rattling her thoughts. The stallion galloped so fast that soon the screams and shrieks from Fiorn faded, becoming fainter the further away they traveled. As she hung from the stranger's lap, she saw only the moonlit blur of jensai blooms, brush, rocks and ground through her curtain of hair.

Cuts on her arms and legs burned, but she knew they were minor. Somehow when the stranger had thrown her out the window, he had kept her from being seriously injured.

The stench of smoke still filled her nostrils and clung to her tresses. The smoke muffled each strand's normally attune senses. It was as though a part of her was blindfolded, unable to clearly see, and she had to struggle to hold back the panic that threatened to overcome her.

Liana tried to calm her thoughts as the horse sped from the seaside village toward the forest. Her belly rocked against the stranger's hard waist and she wondered how she would escape such a powerful man.

Cool evening air caressed her naked buttocks as they traveled. Her breasts rubbed against the man's breeches, her nipples tightening as hard as *ansi* stones. The intimate place between her thighs tingled and grew damp as their bodies moved together on the horse.

Ye, gods. The man had her bound and gagged, and was *kidnapping* her, and she still *wanted* him.

If the hardness against her belly was any indication, the stranger wanted her, too.

Not that she had had any doubt since she had seen the vision of the two of them back in the tavern. Mayhap that was why he had kidnapped her.

But why then had he walked away?

Perhaps he meant to take her to the Sorcerer.

No!

Liana forced her mind away from such a hideous thought and focused on her friends. She was certain Tierra had escaped the fire since she was home ill in their cottage by the sea.

But Ranelle...no matter what her own destiny was, Liana had to know Ranelle's fate. If she concentrated, she should be able to discern whether or not her heart-sister still lived.

Soul heavy with fear for her friend, Liana did her best to relax her body and slide into a trance. She blocked out everything but her search for the knowledge of what had happened to Ranelle. Searching for her *halia's* lifeforce.

Back, Liana's own lifeforce traveled. Back to the chaos in Fiorn. Where people still shouted and screamed and cried. Not only was the tavern engulfed in fire, but the fishmonger's and the butcher's, too.

Soon the whole village might be aflame.

A twinge of empathy gripped Liana, sadness for any lives that might have been lost in such tragedy. But she felt no such compassion for the place where she had been abandoned at birth. Where all but Ranelle and Tierra, her heart-sisters, had treated her as an outsider from the time of her arrival. The whole of Fiorn could burn to the ground for all Liana cared, as long as her friends were safe.

Circling above the village, massive winged beasts appeared to be searching for something...beasts like the one that had grabbed Liana's wrist at the tavern.

She shuddered at the thought, and again turned her thoughts to her *halia*. Ranelle was all that mattered now, and Liana knew with certainty that her heart-sister wasn't there. She was nowhere to be found in Fiorn.

Liana choked back a sob at the absence of her *halia's* lifeforce. Could Ranelle be...dead?

But wait. Liana's consciousness grasped a thread of hope. Her essence followed the feeling. Farther away, along the shore...she saw Ranelle fleeing, stumbling over a log on the sand. Her heart-sister was alive!

Liana frowned when she realized Ranelle's dress was in shreds, and she might as well have been naked. Her golden skin shimmered in the moonlight, her large, firm breasts bounced as she ran, her mahogany tresses floating behind her in the wind. Ranelle paused to look behind her, and as she turned Liana saw the dark triangle of hair between Ranelle's thighs.

Then Liana caught the awareness of something—or someone—following her heart-sister. Liana's skin chilled as she struggled to find out what could be chasing Ranelle.

Before Liana could determine if the being pursuing Ranelle was evil, a sensation on her backside brought Liana out of her trance.

She blinked, again seeing through her curtain of hair bits of moonlit ground flashing by as the horse galloped farther from Fiorn. The gag in her mouth remained, but felt as though it had loosened. Her body rocked against the stranger's...

And she realized his calloused hand was stroking her naked hips, just below her bound hands.

He was touching her almost reverently.

"*Zjenni*." The stranger groaned as though he was in mortal pain as his palm caressed her buttocks, sliding over each smooth cheek.

Liana's eyes widened and she caught her breath as the man moved his hand. Her core ached with wanting as he fondled her, his palm sliding down her thighs to behind her knees, and back to her hips.

"Sweet *zjenni*," he murmured, his words deep and throaty as his knuckles grazed her backside. "So beautiful. So soft."

The timber of his voice set Liana on fire. It was rich and sensual. And when he eased his hand down the crevice of her buttocks, lower and lower yet, she nearly came undone. Her heart pounded hard and fast. She barely noticed the movement of the horse beneath their bodies as the stranger's fingertips brushed the tangle of curls between her thighs and teased her clit.

Liana trembled, a moan rising in her throat behind the cloth in her mouth. The man's woodsy scent surrounded her, fueling her desire for him. In the back of her mind she knew she should fight the erotic sensations, but she was powerless to stop them — and she wanted him too badly.

She closed her eyes as the stranger's fingers slid into her slick quim, and she grew impossibly wetter yet.

The man thrust one finger deep inside her. "Gods. You are so tight." He groaned again as he rammed deep, down to his knuckles and back out again.

His finger was so big, and she was so small, that Liana would have cried out from the surprise of the sensation if it were not for the binding in her mouth. She moaned as he continued to move his finger in and out, matching the rhythm of the horse's gallop. Before she realized what she was doing, Liana found herself instinctively rocking against his hand, raising her hips on his thighs, begging without words for more.

She felt his other arm move, and then the horse's reins fell across her back. In the next instant, as he continued to thrust his finger inside her, the stranger yanked her gown up higher, above her breasts with his free hand. He then slid his hand beneath her and onto her breast. The contact of his hot palm nearly drove her wild as he kneaded her nipple. Liana couldn't believe how erotic it felt being stroked and touched as she lay bound across the stranger's lap.

"Come for me, *zjenni*," he all but growled. "I want to see you climax. I want to *feel* it."

The stranger's motions intensified, and the sensations within Liana grew. So powerful, so unbelievable. Again the vision filled her mind of his massive body sliding between her thighs and into her moist slit. Their slick, naked skin as they pressed their bodies together, his broad chest rubbing against her nipples. Her legs wrapping around his waist as he thrust his cock inside her, again and again.

Liana's muscles tensed, and in the next moment a muffled scream rose behind her gag as an orgasm ripped through her body. Brilliant flashes exploded behind her eyes, blinding her in their intensity. Her breathing grew hard and ragged, a fine sheen of perspiration coating her skin as tremors shook her body.

"Yes. *Yes, zjenni,*" he whispered as the spasms continued to grip her.

But the stranger did not stop. As the horse raced through the forest, the man continued teasing the nub between her thighs, and thrusting his fingers inside her core until she climaxed again.

And yet again.

Until her body was limp with exhaustion. Until she slid into a deep sleep.

* * * * *

When Aric realized Liana had fallen asleep, he reluctantly removed his fingers from between her thighs. He caressed her buttocks with his palm as he drew in a shuddering breath.

"Ah, *zjenni,*" he murmured, again uttering the Nordain word that meant *most precious.* His cock ached so badly to fuck the maiden that he feared he might spill his seed in his breeches.

As Baethel entered the D'euan Forest, Aric took his hand from Liana's breast. He gripped the reins tight in one hand while his other continued to stroke Liana's hips.

The dappled stallion would reach the Bewitching Pool with no need for guidance from Aric. Yet he clung to the straps as if they might help him rein in the urge to stop the horse's flight—and then take the Tanzinite maid on the forest floor.

Prophecy be damned.

No! He would not betray his people by mating with a Tanzinite female. It was against everything he had been trained to believe in since the time of his birth. He was Aric L'tiercel, King of the Nordain.

A man of power.

And she, the wingless Tanzinite...

By the gods, what had possessed him to touch her, to bring Liana to climax? When he had viewed her naked buttocks across his lap, it was as though his hand had a will of its own. And once he had caressed her silken skin — he had been lost to the sensation of feeling her intimately. He had recalled the exquisite look of rapture on her face when he had watched her from her window, and he had wanted to see her experience such pleasure again.

Aric slid his dagger out and carefully cut at the cloth that gagged Liana. He had only put it on her to keep her from alerting the irani of their whereabouts. With one hand he slit the strap binding her wrists, then re-sheathed his dagger. Carefully he massaged her wrists, hoping that he had not bound her hands too tightly. Her skin was so soft, so delicate.

His hand traveled from her wrists, again to her bare buttocks, and a long, shuddering sigh issued from him. The ache in his cock had only grown more intense, and there was naught he could do to relieve his need.

Aric clenched his jaw and forced himself to yank the maid's clothing down, over her breasts and hips. It was difficult, given her position on his lap, but he managed. The sheer material did little good, as even in the barest of moonlight creeping through the trees, he could still see her fair skin, still see the crevice of her smooth buttocks.

He could imagine just how sweet the nectar from her quim would taste. Almost without thought, he moved his hand to his mouth and licked her juice from his fingers. He closed his eyes, savoring her unique flavor on his tongue.

Lord Ir.

Biting back a curse, Aric snapped his eyes open and grabbed Baethel's reins with both hands. He forced his gaze to the canopy of trees overhead and the patches of night sky visible through the forest. Long ago his keen senses had told him they had managed to escape the irani without detection.

But what had happened to Jalen and Renn? If any being could find them, it was Toen the Overseer, who traveled most often in the form of a white wolf. On rare occasions the Overseer took other forms, including that of a white raven. Aric expected Toen to arrive soon with news of Renn's and Jalen's whereabouts.

Aric sighed and shook his head, trying to clear his thoughts. For now it did no good to be concerned for his brother and his friend. It would take all his focus and will to protect the Tanzinite maid from the Sorcerer.

To protect Liana from himself.

And to protect his people from the prophecy.

Chapter Three

When Baethel reached a moonlit meadow at the outskirts of the D'euan Forest, Aric bade the horse to stop. If it were not for Baethel's keen night vision, they never could have traveled as far — the vegetation grew so densely in places that once the sun sank behind the Phoenician Range, a man could not see his hand before his face.

Aric slid Liana from his lap so that she was hanging facedown over the horse's withers, and then he managed to dismount without disturbing her sleep. As he lifted her from Baethel's back, Liana's sweet scent of jensai blooms enveloped him. Her feminine form was soft and warm in his arms, sending a sharp sensation straight to his nether regions.

Twigs snapped and leaves crunched beneath Aric's boots as he carried her across the clearing to where they would make camp. The meadow was almost bright as day, the silvery light of the moon giving an enchanted glow to their surroundings. In the distance he heard the musical sound of the Everlasting River as it rushed along, swollen with melting snows from the Phoenicians. Just over a rise was the Elvin Bewitching Pool, where Aric would take Liana on the morrow to bathe.

And perhaps she would tell him of Jalen's and Renn's whereabouts using her Seer's skills and the magic of the pool.

Just the thought of seeing Liana naked as she washed her fair skin was enough to set Aric's teeth on edge. He would have to leave her to bathe on her own.

He shook his head. No, if Liana still feared him, she might flee into the forest, and who knew what dangers might be waiting for her.

Or, despite his precautions, they may have been followed by one of the Sorcerer's minions.

Aric released a sigh of longing as he settled Liana on a bed of thick pine needles and leaves. He tucked a strand of hair behind her delicately pointed ear, and could not help but smile at the contented look upon her face as she slept. A woman sated by multiple orgasms, she would probably rest well through the night.

He, on the other hand, was less likely to find such peaceful oblivion.

Aric forced himself to walk away from Liana to the horse. He removed Baethel's halter and saddlebags, brushed the stallion's dappled gray coat until it shined, and then left Baethel to graze.

After Aric gathered dry firewood and built a fire within a ring of stones, he withdrew a blanket from the saddlebags. His gut clenched, concern gnawing at him, as he wondered where Jalen and Renn could be. Since Aric's parents' deaths, and the loss of their brother and younger sister, Aric and Renn had no family save each other. And Jalen had become like a brother to them both, too.

Hopefully Toen had located the men and the three would arrive soon. No matter his fierce loyalty to his people. No matter his determination to avoid the pleasures he knew he would find within Liana's welcoming warmth. Aric L'tiercel, King of the Nordain, actually *feared* remaining alone in the Tanzinite maid's presence longer than required.

She might be forbidden, but she was a temptation he was afraid even he could not resist.

But resist he would.

The future of his people depended upon it.

Aric laid the blanket in the clearing, and then carefully moved Liana onto it. As he settled her onto her back, her lips parted and a slight moan eased through.

Mesmerized, Aric watched as Liana shifted, her arm sliding from her belly to her side, her sheer clothing pulling taut across her breasts. He watched her nipples bead, as though she was aware of his perusal, and he didn't know whether to curse or thank the gods for this moonlit night.

All reason left him as he stared at her hardened nipples.

Just one taste.

As long as he did not mate with Liana, he rationalized, his people were safe from the prophecy.

Yes. He would just taste her.

He leaned forward and licked one peak through the thin fabric, and it grew even tauter yet. Before he realized what he was doing, Aric had moved his mouth to her other nipple, licking and sucking.

Liana moaned and arched her back, but he could tell she still slept. Perhaps dreaming of him filling her. Need grew within Aric, fast and furious, and it was all he could do to hold himself back. His cock was so hard he felt sure he could bore a hole through a plank with it.

Several planks.

Half out of his mind with lust, Aric yanked Liana's gown up over her breasts and then groaned at the sight of her naked body. How beautiful she was. Her alabaster skin glowed in the moonlight, her nipples hard and begging for his mouth. Her silvery-white hair shimmered and almost seemed to move, like a glistening waterfall.

Still fuily clothed, Aric pressed Liana's legs apart and knelt between her bare thighs. Lord Ir, but he ached to enter her, to fuck her sweet quim until she screamed with her climax.

Aric leaned over Liana, bracing one hand on the blanket beside her. Barely breathing, he traced the tip of his finger down her cheek. Gods, but her skin was so soft. He continued, over her parted lips, over the gown bunched above her breasts, to one nipple. Sweat beaded on his forehead as he stroked her delicate skin. He cupped her perfect globe, flicking the pearl tip with his thumb, and groaned in agony.

Why could she not be a Nordain maiden? Why did she have to be a Tanzinite and the one woman he was not allowed to possess?

Liana moaned again, and Aric felt a gentle movement across the hand he had braced on the blanket. He glanced down at her hair.

And saw that it was moving. Caressing him.

Stunned, Aric watched as her tresses slid across his skin. Was it his imagination? Was it a breeze causing her hair to move? Yet he felt no wind.

"Please… " Liana murmured, drawing his attention back to her face.

Her eyes were closed, and he knew she still dreamed. But then her eyelids fluttered, and opened, and her gaze locked with his.

And he became lost in those depths, the color of the Mairi Sea.

"Who..." Her voice wavered. She sucked in her breath, causing her breasts to rise. "Who are you?"

"Aric," he whispered and then captured her mouth with his.

He kissed her, a long, slow, and sensual kiss. At first Liana was hesitant, but then seemed to become as lost in the sensation as he. He moved his lips over hers, then eased his tongue inside her mouth, reveling in the sweet taste of her. His cock pressed against his breeches, and he lowered himself between her thighs, rubbing his hardness along her naked mound.

Liana fisted her hands in his tunic, clinging to him while he kissed her, as though she feared drowning. Tentatively her tongue met his, and then her kiss grew bolder as she followed his lead, thrusting that sweet tongue inside his mouth.

Her hair continued to move, caressing him, and he wondered how it might feel if he were to lay naked with Liana. To have her hair sliding across his bare chest as she climbed on top of him and rode him hard and fast.

"No," he muttered against her lips. "Mustn't..."

Yet he couldn't control himself. It was as though he was intoxicated by Liana, drunk beyond reason.

"You taste of heaven," he murmured as he eased lower, lapping at the salty skin between her breasts.

She thrust her hands into his hair, gripping him as he suckled each nipple. "Don't stop—" she begged when he removed his mouth from her breasts.

Aric slid his tongue down Liana's belly toward the soft triangle of sea foam curls. Her woman's scent made his cock harder yet. "Say my name," he demanded.

"Don't stop...*Aric.*" Liana buried her hands in his hair and pulled his face down between her thighs. "Do *not* stop!"

He smiled as he settled between her legs. "My pleasure, sweet one." He gripped her thighs with his hands, spreading her wider, and placed his mouth on her clit and sucked.

"I—*oh, my gods,*" she cried, and then bucked her hips as he licked her excited nub and slid a finger into her quim. She was so hot, so wet and so ready for him. He could imagine how good it would feel to be inside her, how it would feel to fuck her again and again.

And he cursed fate that it was not to be.

Aric lapped at her clit while he thrust his finger in and out of her tight quim, mimicking the movement he would like to be making with his rock-hard cock. Yes, he had been right. She tasted like the nectar of the gods must taste. And the scent of her arousal was heaven indeed.

"Come for me again, *zjenni,*" he murmured against her luscious folds. "Come for me."

Liana arched her back, clenched her hands tighter in his hair and clamped her legs hard around him. In the next instant her body corded, and she screamed and thrashed as she came.

When the last tremor faded from her orgasm, Aric rose up so that he was again above her, his hands at either side of her slender body.

Gods, she was beautiful. He swallowed hard as he watched Liana. His arms trembled from the force he exerted in holding himself back from unlacing his breeches and taking her.

Liana's breathing came shallow as she stared up at Aric, her breasts rising and falling. With one hand he eased her clothing down, covering her nakedness.

Tracing his finger along Liana's pert nose, Aric murmured, "Sleep, *zjenni*."

"But—" Liana started, a puzzled expression upon her face.

Aric placed his fingers on her lips and almost groaned at the thought of that generous mouth on his cock, sucking him dry.

Liana continued to stare up at him, until a long, shuddering sigh took hold of her. A few moments later her eyelids fluttered shut and then Aric eased from between her legs. He covered her with a light blanket from his saddlebags, and then sat beside her, watching and waiting until he was positive she had fallen asleep.

With a muffled curse, he got to his feet, turned his back on Liana and walked to the edge of the meadow. He unlaced his breaches, releasing his throbbing cock. Tipping his head back, Aric closed his eyes and stroked his cock, imagining that he was plunging into Liana's hot depths, fucking her mercilessly. Ramming into her hard and fast as she watched him thrust, hearing her scream with pleasure when her orgasm wracked her body.

Aric bit back a cry as he came, spilling his seed onto the bark of a tree.

When he had returned to his senses, he realized that relieving his discomfort had done little to alleviate his need. He now wanted Liana more than ever.

By the gods, this obsession would be the ruin of him.

After whistling a command to Baethel, telling the stallion to stand guard over Liana, Aric transformed into his nordai form and took to the skies. The wind felt good in his feathers as he spread his wings and glided over the dark forest. He pumped his wings, harder and harder, trying to work out his frustrations.

He patrolled the moonlit night, searching for any sign that the Sorcerer's minions had followed them. Searching for signs of Jalen, Renn, and Toen the Overseer.

Searching for answers to the odd feeling growing in his heart and gripping his soul.

But the wind refused to give up the answers he sought.

* * * * *

"*Zjenni.*" A husky whisper called Liana from her sleep.

"No," she mumbled, not wanting to wake. Wanting to enjoy the dream of being cradled and loved by the dark stranger. Her tresses moved, caressing her shoulders, trailing across her breasts. And in her dream, her hair slid across the arms of the man holding her, stroking him the way he had stroked her.

"Wake, *zjenni,*" a low voice murmured, and then firm lips moved along the curve of her ear to its tip.

Liana startled. Her tresses went still and her eyelids flew open to find that she was indeed in the arms of her dream man, lying next to him on a blanket. The same man who had kidnapped her, and then touched her as no one had ever before. The dark stranger's woodsy male scent surrounded her as she blinked up at him, and her foggy senses recalled last eve.

A fleeting smile crossed Aric's face as her gaze met his.

Aric. She remembered that he had insisted she call him by name when she had begged him to continue pleasuring her. Liana flushed with embarrassment from the tips of her ears to the bottom of her toes at the memory of her wanton demands of this handsome man, and at the thought of his tongue on her nub and in her quim.

Raising her chin, Liana attempted to pull away from him. "Release me," she insisted, and was infuriated at how small and afraid her voice sounded.

Aric grinned as he gently ran one finger down her nose to the end, a deep chuckle rumbling within his massive chest. "So brave for one so tiny."

Glaring, Liana tried to draw back, despite the fact there was nowhere for her to go. "Do *not* touch me."

"You did not mind my touch last night." A wicked glint appeared in his black eyes, and his voice was deep and sensual. "You seemed to enjoy it, if I recall. In fact, I distinctly remember you *demanding* my attentions."

Cheeks burning at the thought, and the memory of his face between her thighs and his tongue licking her clit, Liana tried to muster her dignity. It was not easy while lying flat on her back, in the arms of the man who had tasted her quim intimately.

She struggled for a retort, and instead voiced the fear in her heart. "Do you mean to take me to Zanden?"

A cloud passed over Aric's features, a dark thunderstorm of anger. "I saved you from the bastard."

His jaw clenched and his eyes flashed. "The irani had come for you."

Liana blinked, unable to keep the surprise from her voice. "Who are you, then? Why have you taken me? Why would you want to help me?"

The man shifted her from his embrace, clasping his large hands around her slender waist and moving her further away from him on the blanket. "As I told you, I am Aric." In a fluid motion that reminded her of a graceful forest creature, he rose to his feet and scowled down at her. His features hardened, and no longer did he seem gentle or caring. No, his eyes had turned cold and indifferent, like a bird of prey's. "It is my sworn duty to keep you from Sorcerer Zanden."

"*Duty?*" Liana cocked an eyebrow as she raised herself to a sitting position on the blanket. "And was it your *duty* to touch me in such a manner?"

She could almost swear she saw his cheeks redden as he replied, "A mistake that must not be repeated."

Mistake?

Before she could respond, Aric spun on his heel and strode to a smoldering fire within a circle of rocks in the clearing. Flames popped and crackled, and Liana noticed for the first time that what looked like a giant potato was roasting on a spit over the fire. Her stomach rumbled as she caught a whiff of the delicious smell and her mouth watered.

Confusion swirled through Liana as she watched Aric crouch down to rustle through a saddlebag. Muscles rippled along his powerful arms as he withdrew several items, unwrapped and laid them onto a piece of cloth. A loaf of bread, a wheel of cheese and dried figs.

She forced her gaze away from Aric and studied her surroundings. They were in the middle of a dense wood, a part of a forest so thick that the morning sunlight barely made it through the canopy above. No longer did she smell the ocean or the filth of the village. Instead she breathed in the crisp scent of pine, the rich smell of loam and the unmistakable perfume of jensai blooms. In the distance she heard a river's roar as it rushed through the forest.

In her almost twenty seasons, it was the first time she had ever been away from Fiorn, the only home she had ever known.

A black feather on the blanket caught her attention, and she ran her finger along its soft length as her thoughts turned to Ranelle and Tierra. Liana wondered how her friends fared, and her belly twisted at the thought of either of them being captured by Zanden's minions.

Liana toyed with the black feather as she debated on whether or not to try to find her friends with her essence again, but Aric grunted, drawing her gaze back to him. His black hair brushed his shoulders as he slid the roasted vegetable from the spit, onto the cloth beside the other food. The stubble on his face was longer this morn, making him seem even more untamed.

Her heart pounded faster as she thought about his hands upon her flesh. Vividly she recalled his suckling her breasts, and then the feel of his stubble scraping the inside of her thighs as he licked her clit. To her dismay, her nipples hardened and she felt a sharp ache below.

Aric turned back to her, carrying an assortment of food. Liana dropped the feather and quickly crossed her arms over her breasts, attempting to hide the evidence of her desire for him—but she was too late. She saw his throat work as he swallowed and stared at her arms that now hid her swollen nipples. His gaze dropped to her lap, and she flushed anew as she realized that through the sheer garment he could easily see the triangle of hair between her thighs.

After what seemed an eternity, Aric seemed to regain his composure. He reached her in a couple of strides. "Eat," he commanded as he set the food on the blanket beside her.

Certainly a man accustomed to giving orders, she thought as she glared at him. Well, she was not one to easily take orders, which was something he would soon learn. However, considering she had not eaten for several hours, she decided to ignore the flare of irritation and break her fast.

They ate in silence. The only sounds around them were the rush of a river in the distance, chattering squirrels and raven cries. Liana was so ravenous that even the dry traveler's bread tasted delicious. The potato was roasted to perfection, and the cheese and dried figs rounded out the meal nicely.

Aric slid a dagger from a sheath at his side and sliced another hunk of cheese from the wheel. On his weapon, a blood red ruby glittered in the sunlight.

Where had she seen a dagger like the one he had? More than likely she had noticed him wearing the weapon in the tavern, but was too rattled by his watching her to have paid much attention to it.

She wondered why he had not cooked a fowl instead of a vegetable, or added dried venison to their breakfast as was common in Fiorn. Considering she did not believe in eating any of the gods' creatures, Liana was pleased that Aric had not added such awful fare to their meal.

While she chewed her food, she tried to concentrate on her meal and avoid Aric's lustful expression as he stared at her body. She felt naked in the sheer garment, and wished she had her cloak, or that she was wearing one of the woolen shifts she preferred to don when not working. She had always hated the transparent fabric of the costume Nira had forced Liana, Ranelle and Tierra to wear whenever they worked at the tavern. And Liana hated the way men had ogled her body as she told fortunes.

Yet...truth be told, she did not *really* mind *Aric's* stare. She realized that she almost welcomed it. Then it occurred to her that the sensation made her feel *powerful*.

And she wondered what she might do with that power.

Liana raised her eyes from her bread and watched as Aric took a swig of water and then passed the flask to her. As she put her lips to the opening, her gaze locked with his. The cool water slid over her tongue, and she remembered how he had kissed her last night, the feel of his mouth on hers, and the elemental taste of him.

She wanted to taste him again.

All of him.

He clenched his fist and hardened his jaw, looking as though he had been able to read her most intimate thoughts. After she had pushed the cork into the flask and set it on the blanket, Aric grasped Liana by her upper arms, bringing her up with him to stand.

"We shall go to the pool and you shall bathe now," he said in that commanding tone that irked her to no end.

Liana scowled up at him. "You have no right to order me to do anything."

"You *will* do as I say." Before she realized what he was doing, Aric grabbed her around the waist and threw her over one powerful shoulder as though she was naught more than a child. Over his other shoulder he slung his saddlebag that he had snatched up from beside the horse.

Furious, Liana pounded his back with her fists. "Let me down!"

Aric chuckled and settled his hand upon her buttocks as he strode through the forest. Squirrels chattered and blackbirds cried out, but the sounds faded as Liana became intensely aware of the heat of his palm radiating through her thin gown.

Gods, she wanted him to touch her again. She wanted more than his hand caressing her, and his mouth between her thighs.

She wanted him *inside* her.

When they reached a hidden pool, Aric carefully set Liana down on a crumbling set of stone stairs. For a moment she forgot to be angry with him. She drew in a deep breath and gazed about her, enchanted by the magic of the place. It was too beautiful for words.

Massive oaks and pines stood sentinel around a glistening sapphire pool. Sunshine swirled through the canopy of trees, dust motes dancing within the shafts of light.

Giant jensai blooms grew in clusters, their emerald vines twisting around the trees. Liana had never seen such enormous jensai — easily as large as a man's head, when the norm was the size of her palm. Even their crimson color was more vivid and their scent sweeter than normal.

It was heady, intoxicating. And like all jensai, certainly too potent and dangerous to touch.

Liana's gaze returned to the pool. She longed to slip into the waters and cleanse the smoke from her hair so that she might fully feel all there was to enjoy in this charmed place.

Liana looked up at Aric. "Where are we?"

He shrugged. "At the Elvin Bewitching Pool."

With a gasp, she widened her eyes. "I thought stories of the pool were but Elvin tales."

A smile quirked the corner of Aric's mouth. "It is as real and as magical as the tales say."

"I can feel it." Even though her senses were muted, her tresses vibrated as they soaked in the otherworldly air.

"Now get into the pool and bathe," Aric commanded, folding his arms across his chest.

That feeling of power rose within Liana. Despite her own desire to cleanse herself, she raised her chin and shook her head. "I will not."

Aric growled, and in the next moment Liana yelped as he yanked her gown over her head, leaving her naked before him. She started to cover herself, but instead she decided that if he was going to play rough, she would, too.

Liana straightened, holding her shoulders back, keeping her hands at her sides. Aric's growl turned into a groan as he stared at her breasts. The heat of his gaze caused her nipples to harden, and it was all Liana could do to hold back a moan.

"You will get into the pool and bathe," he demanded again, but his voice was rough and it wavered. "Before I take you there myself."

A delicious feeling of wickedness overcame Liana and she had to restrain a smile. "I answer to no man."

Aric pulled his tunic over his head and then began untying his breeches. "You *will* answer to me."

Chapter Four

Aric dropped his sheathed dagger onto the shore beside his tunic. He stripped off his boots and breeches, tossing them aside in his haste, but he never took his eyes off Liana.

He was strong. He was King of the Nordain. He could fight the temptation to bury himself in this beautiful naked woman.

Liana clenched her small fists and glared at Aric defiantly.

Yes. He definitely *had* to teach the maid a lesson.

She yelped as Aric swept her in his arms, and he tried not to groan from the pleasure of feeling her skin against his.

"Let me go!" she shouted as he slowly strode down the ancient steps.

"You will learn to obey me," he growled, and then tossed her toward the center of the chilly pool.

Eyes wide with shock, Liana screamed, and then in the next moment she vanished beneath the crystal water. She resurfaced, sputtering and cursing. "You son of an irani!"

Aric covered his mouth with one hand, trying to hold back a grin at the sight of her enraged pixie face.

Splashing, Liana struggled to stand and then moved closer to him, where the water was to her waist. Her skin pebbled with gooseflesh and her nipples hardened from the cold water. "No, an irani is too good for *you*." Her pale tresses hung in wet ropes around her face. She clenched her jaw, her eyes spitting fury. "You are no better than the dung of that hateful beast!"

Aric couldn't help a chuckle. Mirth rose within him until he was laughing so hard that his sides ached.

"You—you—" Liana marched up to him, her hands clenched.

The thought of her tiny fists attempting to hurt him, made Aric laugh all the harder.

And then she flattened her palms against his chest and shoved with all her might.

Caught unawares, Aric stumbled back in the water. One foot slipped on a moss-covered stone—he lost his balance and toppled over.

He flailed, and the next thing he knew he was beneath the icy surface, his nose and mouth filling with water. He sprang to his feet, coughing and choking, ready to teach the Tanzinite maid another lesson—

Only to see her giggling.

Her sea green eyes were bright with laughter, making her beyond beautiful. All Aric wanted to do then was kiss her.

One kiss.

"Come here, woman," he demanded.

Liana shook her head, a smile still on her lips. "No."

In one long stride he reached her. He grabbed her, pinning her arms to her sides. Her laughter died and her pupils dilated as he pulled her soft form against his muscled body. His cock hardened despite the water's chill, and he pressed it tight to her belly.

She gasped and her lips parted, and Aric couldn't restrain himself any longer. He swooped down, taking possession of her mouth. Slowly he moved his lips over hers, then slid his tongue into the warm recesses. Liana moaned into his mouth, her tongue gently mating with his, until the kiss became frantic, their mutual need building and building.

"Sweet *zjenni*," he murmured as sensations whirled through him. The taste of her, the feel of her nipples against his chest, her womanly scent mixed with the heady perfume of the jensai...it was too much.

Just as Aric broke the kiss and grasped Liana around the waist to raise her up, ready to impale her womanhood with his cock—he came to his senses.

He froze, for a moment unable to move, fearing that he would take her and damn the consequences.

Gods, no.

His people. How could he forget them? How could he betray them?

"No," Aric roared and pushed Liana away from him, toward the center of the pool. She stumbled back in the water and stared up at him, her features etched with confusion—and hurt.

In that instant he could see the pain and humiliation in her expression. After being abandoned by her own people, after a lifetime of being scorned and maligned, she thought that he, too, was rejecting her.

Liana raised her chin and crossed her arms over her chest, and turned her back on him.

Aric's heart twisted and he moved so close that there was but a hair's breadth between him and Liana. "*Zjenni*," he murmured.

"Leave." The word sounded low and sorrowful coming from her lips, and he heard the ache in her voice as she continued, "I will bathe as you wish. Just leave me be."

"It is not as you think." Aric placed his hands on her small shoulders and his gut clenched when he felt her flinch. "Do you think I do not want you?" He pressed his throbbing erection against her buttocks and groaned. "I want you more than any woman I have ever known."

Liana sniffed, and he feared she was crying. "Why then did you push me away?"

"I—" He paused, unsure of how much to tell her. "It is not to be."

"Because of who I am." Her voice was mocking. "The Tanzinite woman who was discarded by her own kind for her imperfections."

"No, *zjenni*." Aric grasped her shoulders and spun her around. Her eyes widened as he held her tight against him. "I watched you in Fiorn for far longer than you know. I have seen all that you are." His eyes held hers as he tried to make her understand. "You are grace and beauty. You are kind, generous and loving. You are perfect. You are everything I have ever wanted in a mate."

Aric's heart ached as he realized the truth in his own words. "But I cannot have you because of who *I* am."

She sighed and looked down at the water, and trailed her finger along its surface. "I do not understand, but I thank you for the kind words."

"Liana." He caught her chin in his hand and tilted her head up. "I speak truth." And with that he gave her a gentle kiss and then released her.

Aware of her gaze following him, Aric moved to the edge of the pool, reached for his saddlebags and retrieved the flask of cleansing gel. When he returned to Liana, he took her in his arms and carefully leaned her back so that her flaxen hair became saturated again. He stood her up and poured some of the gel onto his hand. Leaving the flask to float on top of the water, he began massaging the soap into her tresses.

Aric could almost swear that he felt a sigh reverberating through her wet hair as he cleansed it. The gel smelled of almonds, its scent mingling with Liana's sweet perfume. When he finished, he leaned her back again, rinsing the soap from her hair.

Once he had again retrieved the flask and squeezed more gel into his palm, Aric began soaping Liana's body, taking care not to rub too hard in the places where she had been scraped during their escape. Aric frowned at the sight of the red marks against the pale skin of her wrists. Almost without thought he lifted both wrists to his lips and kissed them, one at a time.

Liana moaned and tilted her head back, her breasts jutting forward. Aric became lost in the sensations of washing her, moving his hands to the soft white globes, enjoying the sight of his tanned skin against her pale flesh. He reveled in the feel of her soap-slick breasts against his palms. Aric rinsed the soap away, dripping handfuls of the crystal water over her front, noting that her nipples were so hard they all but cried out for his mouth to taste them.

He knew he was not allowed to find his release within Liana's body, but he *could* pleasure her again. He moved to the edge of the pool, where the water came to his knees. Her eyes widened as he placed her on the steps so that she was a good two feet higher, almost as tall as he.

"What are you doing?" she asked, then gasped when Aric lowered his head and lapped at her nipple. With a groan, he captured the nub between his lips and began sucking and fondling her, moving from one breast to the other. She cried out and slid her hands into his hair, pulling his head tighter to her breasts.

"Pleasuring you, my sweet *zjenni*." He eased one hand between her thighs and thrust his finger inside her slit, then rubbed her swollen clit.

"*Please*," Liana cried as his motions intensified and his mouth suckled her nipples harder. "*Aric!*" The sound of his name on her lips was like the most potent of wines. "I *need* you inside."

Yes—he could picture himself spreading her thighs and thrusting his cock into her hot quim. Over and over again he would fuck her, spilling his seed in her core.

"Oh, my gods," she screamed as her orgasm took hold, her body shuddering with one aftershock after another until she collapsed against him.

Aric's cock throbbed painfully, and he gritted his teeth as he held Liana in his arms. He would *not* take her. Would not betray his people. He closed his eyes, willing the sensation to lessen, but if anything, it only grew in intensity and he trembled with lust for this fair maid.

Liana moved out of his embrace, and then warmth slid over his cock.

Aric's eyes flew open and he saw her on her knees before him, her mouth enveloping his thick shaft. She gazed up at him as she moved her hand along his bollocks and sucked his hard length.

The sight and the feel of his cock in her mouth was almost too much to bear, and he had to struggle not to come at once.

She pulled away. "Does that not please you?"

"Gods, *yes*," he groaned. How could such an innocent creature know exactly how to touch him?

Liana smiled and took him into her velvet warmth again. Her mouth, so hot, so wet. Her hands fondling his bollocks and then stroking his cock in rhythm with her movements.

Aric was lost. He grasped her head as she eased up and down his shaft, his hands buried in her wet hair. He thrust into her mouth, thrusting into her as he wanted to thrust into her virginity, but could not.

She took him, measure for measure, licking and sucking his cock until he came in a rush. Like a mighty bull, a bellow tore from his throat as the seed burst from his staff and into Liana's mouth. Still she sucked him until he was dry and she had swallowed every drop.

Liana made hungry purring sounds, as though she couldn't get enough of his cock or his seed. She didn't let up, even after the last of his semen was spent. Her fingers continued to move, caressing him, taunting him. Heat filled Aric as she continued her sensual assault.

Like lava within Mount Taka, Aric's lust rose and rose. He filled her mouth again, wanting naught more than to plumb her tight quim. His orgasm erupted through him like the fiery volcano and he spewed his seed into Liana's enchanting mouth.

And then, by gods, he hardened again.

* * * * *

The morning sun had eased high overhead, and Liana snuggled against Aric as they lay sated beside the Bewitching Pool. It had been hours since breakfast, and her stomach growled its demand for food. She could hardly believe that only last eve this man had kidnapped her from the village, and now she was lying in his arms.

Aric snored softly while her head rested upon his chest, her leg straddling his waist, his cock hard against her thigh. A keen sense of pleasure flowed through her, knowing that he still wanted her even after she had brought him to orgasm and swallowed his salty-sweet seed three times. One right after the other.

Still Liana did not understand why Aric refused to enter her, but for now she would not let that dim her enjoyment of this man.

The feelings stirring within her were overwhelming, yet intoxicating.

She had known him for such a short time, but it felt as though he had been in her heart forever. His presence drew at her woman's core and she wanted him in a primal way. But she reveled in the times he had smiled, in the moments he had shown such caring and concern for her.

Liana's tresses had dried, and they caressed Aric's chest and her own nipples. She sighed at the feel of him, amplified by the heightened senses of her hair.

Now that it was clean, her hair absorbed Elvin magic from the Bewitching Pool. With her increased awareness, Liana fully understood what she must do next, even though Aric had spoken naught of it.

She lightly stroked his hair from his brow, and discovered that a raven's black feather had landed in the soft strands. After setting the feather aside, Liana eased away from Aric, careful not to disturb his sleep. Somehow the magic of the place had allowed his warrior's senses to relax—he was resting as peaceful as a babe who had just suckled his mother's breast.

A breeze caressed Liana's naked skin as she walked down the ancient and crumbling steps, into the pool. Her hair danced and sang on the light wind, absorbing energy from all of nature. Energy that was needed for the constant renewal of Liana's lifeforce.

All was silent in the forest, as though waiting. The only sound was the gentle sloshing against her thighs as she walked deeper and deeper into the pool, until the water teased her breasts.

Crisp air filled her lungs, and the rich perfume of the jensai. Liana allowed her essence to seep into the Bewitching Pool, opening herself to whatever message the waters had to offer. An eerie emerald green began to glow from the normally crystal blue pool, as though light shone up from its depths. Liana closed her eyes, releasing her essence to merge with Elvin magic.

Complete blackness filled her senses, and then a vision began to form.

An image that nearly shocked Liana out of her trance.

In a room filled with gold velvet cushions, Tierra reclined on a chair—completely naked. Her head was thrown back, her red tresses almost reaching the floor. Her breasts jutted forward, her nipples large and hard with arousal. Tierra's long legs were splayed wide, her hands buried in the dark hair of the person between her thighs.

And then Liana realized that it was a woman who pleasured Tierra.

A woman?

Despite her surprise, Liana felt a tingle between her own thighs while she watched Tierra, who moaned as the woman lapped at her nub. And then it was as though Liana could feel the sensations building within her, as though *she* was being licked and sucked, just as Aric had tasted her after they had first arrived in the clearing.

As she would like for him to taste her again.

She watched Tierra move her hands from the woman's hair to cup her own breasts, pulling and twisting at her nipples. Moments later, Tierra cried out, her body shuddering with the power of her orgasm.

And to her incredible surprise, Liana came in sync with Tierra.

Liana barely had time to recover from the orgasm, or to accustom herself to the idea of her friend enjoying sex with a woman, when Tierra's image faded.

A new vision replaced the erotic one of Tierra and the dark haired woman.

Liana was on the rainbow sands beside the Mairi Sea. The familiar scent of the ocean filled her senses as she saw a man crouched on the shore, looking as though he was searching for signs of something—or someone.

Jalen. The man's name was a whisper in her mind. Somehow this man was connected to Aric, and his future was intertwined with hers...and another person whom Liana could not yet see. But it was someone close to her. Ranelle, or perhaps Tierra?

Jalen was a sapphire-eyed, muscle-bound god of a man, and when he stood, Liana realized that he was as tall as Aric. As he wiped sand from his palm onto his breeches, the man's biceps bulged from a sleeveless tunic, and hair the color of sunbeams flowed past his shoulders. He had a glittering symbol on his forehead, and as he brushed an errant strand of hair behind his ear, she saw that the ear was pointed. He was not fair enough to be Tanzinite, and he had no wings—could he be Elvin?

Liana watched as Jalen began to jog along the beach, a warrior's bow strapped to his back, his movements as fluid and effortless as a massive cat. His powerful thighs flexed beneath his tight breeches, his sapphire gaze searching the horizon. What—or whom—did he seek?

Liana caught a flash of white, and then saw a wolf loping behind Jalen—the one Aric had called Toen.

Jalen's image dissolved, and in the next moment Liana's vision took her to the edge of a precipice.

At first she saw naught but miles of green forest below, and in the distance the peak of Mount Taka, a wisp of smoke spiraling from its cavernous mouth. Her heart pounded as she caught sight of a great winged creature. Could it be one of the irani, searching for her?

It came closer, and closer yet, until she realized it was a giant nordai.

Before her very eyes, the raven transformed, shifting into the form of a man and landing at the top of the cliff with masculine grace. He was an enormous man with a feral look in his silvery eyes and a scar across one cheek.

Chills overtook Liana and her stomach clenched as she feared the man might be Zanden. Her visions of the Sorcerer had always been from a distance, thus she had never seen him close enough to clearly discern his features. She only knew that he was powerfully built with long black hair.

And an even blacker soul.

She had to know who this man in her vision was. With all her strength she concentrated, searching for his identity...

Renn. His name was Renn. Relief flowed through Liana, but then she realized this predator of a man could still be one of Zanden's minions.

Renn scowled in Liana's vision, as though he had heard her thoughts. Something flashed at his side, a glitter, somehow familiar, but she couldn't quite place what it was. The knowledge came to her that Renn, like Jalen, was somehow linked to Aric.

Before she had opportunity to explore this realization, the man turned to the sky and she saw ominous winged beasts approaching.

Ice sliced through her veins. It was the irani. Searching for *her*.

The cliff disappeared, and a new vision took place.

This time it was Ranelle that she saw. Fear gripped Liana's heart as she realized her *halia* was chained to a wall, her clothing in shreds. Ranelle's arms were bound overhead, her large breasts partially exposed through the tattered garment, her feet bare.

Tears came to Liana as she saw her friend's tired, dirt-streaked face. Her *halia's* eyes were closed, as though she slept, but then Liana heard hinges squeaking.

Ranelle's eyelids flew open.

A massive figure approached Ranelle from the shadows.

And then Liana heard a scream.

* * * * *

A piercing shriek woke Aric. He bolted to his feet and saw Liana screaming in the midst of the Bewitching Pool. In one fluid movement he snatched his dagger from where it lay beside his breeches, and then he plunged into the pool, reaching Liana within seconds.

He caught her around the waist and grasped her naked body to his, holding his dagger at the ready in his free hand. Aric attempted to locate what had frightened his woman, his gaze searching the pool that now glowed with an uncanny green light.

"What is it?" he demanded, seeing naught in the waters, but refusing to lower his guard.

Liana stiffened, her scream dying in her throat. He glanced down at her beautiful face and saw that her sea green eyes were glazed, unfocused.

She had been in a trance. The knot in his gut lessened a bit, his fear for her subsiding with the knowledge she had not been attacked. Yet concern still gripped him as he wondered what had caused her to scream.

The glow faded from the pool until the waters were crystal blue once again. Slowly Liana's body relaxed, and the light came back into her eyes. She blinked and tears began spilling down her cheeks.

"Do not cry, sweet one." Aric drew Liana against him, careful to keep the dagger away from her fair skin as he held her. "Naught will happen to you as long as I shall live. I promise."

Sobs wracked her slender body as she wrapped her arms around his waist and clung to him. A sense of helplessness washed through Aric and he almost wished that there *had* been some beast for him to slay, something that he could dispatch of to ease whatever troubled her heart and mind.

As Liana's breathing calmed, it occurred to him how terrified *he* had been. Not of any creature. He had been frightened to lose *her*. He had been ready to slay man or beast, or an army if he need be, just to protect his woman.

Ah, gods. Aric sighed as he moved his gaze toward the heavens that were obscured by the thick canopy above. He had thought of Liana as *his* woman from the moment he had flown to her rescue — and he had vowed to protect her as long as he lived.

Just as he had long ago vowed to protect his people.

Aric knew not what to do with his feelings for the Tanzinite maid. The only thing left for him to do was to seek counsel with Dair's wisest beings, and make his decision at that time. But he must hurry and hear their advice before moonchange — for at moonchange he would be relegated to his nordai form.

For now he would do what he could to cherish and protect Liana.

He moved his mouth close to her delicately pointed ear and murmured, "What did you see, *zjenni*?"

Liana shuddered and tipped her tear-streaked face up to his. "Ranelle. My heart-sister. She..." Choking on another sob, Liana paused and then continued, "She was held captive. I — I think the Sorcerer had her."

"The *gishla*?" Aric asked, a new, unexplained rage boiling up within him.

"Yes," Liana whispered. "My visions are usually of future events, but not always." Her voice rose as her words tumbled from her lips in a rush. "I must find her to keep this from happening. I must help her at once!"

Although Aric felt an intense desire to rescue the *gishla*, he shook his head. "No. It is not possible."

Liana's pale face reddened and she tried to push away from Aric, but he refused to release her. "It is my fault the

Sorcerer will try to take Ranelle. If I have to, I will trade my life for hers!"

Aric clenched his jaw and his grip tightened on Liana. "I will die before I see you mated with Zanden."

She stilled. "So I am naught but your *duty*?"

"No. My—" Aric stopped himself. He had almost said, *My love.*

Gritting his teeth, he released his hold on Liana. He took her by the hand and drew her toward the shore. "Come. We need sustenance, and then we can discuss what you saw while in the Bewitching Pool."

Chapter Five

When Liana felt somewhat calmer, and their bellies were full of journey cakes, cheese, and dried apples, Aric bade her to join him on a log beside the smoldering fire. The afternoon sun cast long shadows across the clearing, and squirrels chattered overhead in the pines.

The grass felt cool beneath Liana's bare feet as she walked toward Aric. Baethel whickered as he grazed on the opposite side of the meadow, shaking his head at a swarm of pink and purple butterflies floating by. In the distance the river sounded louder than ever before, rushing through the forest just as blood roared through Liana's veins when she neared the man she had once called stranger.

Aric had dressed in his tunic and breeches, and she had a blanket wrapped around her with a rope cinched about her waist. The blanket was so large on her that she felt as if she were clothed in a tent from a sideshow. He had insisted she cover herself in more than her sheer costume, and she knew it was because he feared he wouldn't be able to rein in his lust if she remained naked, or even semi-naked, in his presence.

Liana seriously considered taking the blanket off, just to torture the man.

With a sigh she settled beside him on the log, and braced her palms against the rough bark. Aric's musky male scent filled her senses, making her long for him more than ever. Once she tasted all of him, once he filled her, would she be satisfied? Or would she crave him even more?

"Before your vision of the *gishla*, what did you see?" Aric asked, his deep voice jolting Liana from her carnal thoughts. His eyes flicked from her to the fire, as though he dared not gaze upon her too long.

Heat rose to her cheeks at the memory of her first vision. "I—I saw my friend Tierra."

Aric's eyes met Liana's "Was she well?"

"Yes." She grew warmer yet as he cocked his brow. "Tierra was enjoying the pleasures of—of a woman."

He smiled and looked at her in a sensual way that made her nipples harden and her body ache for him. "Have you experienced such with a female?" he asked, his voice a husky murmur.

Her eyes widened and her face burned as hot as the cooking fire. "I—I of course not!"

If she did not count having an orgasm while *watching* Tierra and the woman.

Aric captured Liana's chin in his hand, and she caught her breath at the feel of his calloused fingers against her skin. "In some cultures, it is normal for women to enjoy each other in every way. It is considered an extension of their friendship."

Liana barely dared to breathe. She desired for him to kiss her so badly she ached with it. "Friendship?"

He nodded, his face mere fractions from hers. "In the Elvin Kingdom, sensuality between those of both sexes is as natural as the air we breathe. And often expected as a matter of ritual or ceremony."

"It is?" Liana's nipples tightened at the husky sound of Aric's voice, the smell of him and the warmth of his nearness.

He smiled. "Amongst my own people, it is common for men and women to enjoy multiple partners of either sex until they are mated."

"Who are your people?" she whispered.

Aric closed his eyes and inhaled, as though scenting her, imprinting her upon his memory. When he opened his eyes again, he released her chin and leaned forward on the log, facing the fire, his hands clasped between his knees.

Disappointment slid through Liana. She studied her lap and picked at a loose thread on her makeshift clothing as she thought how she would never understand this man. He wanted her, yet he would not touch her. He shut her out, refusing to share anything of his personal life. What was it about him that made her want him so, when all he did was frustrate her?

Liana was tempted to put her hand to his forehead and see what her Seer's sight might tell her, but she reined in the urge. She was almost afraid of what she would learn.

"Tell me what else you saw," he said as he focused intently on the flames.

An errant strand of Liana's hair moved toward Aric. She quickly pushed it over her shoulder and swallowed. "A man named Jalen."

Aric's head snapped up and he suddenly became alert and predatory again. "Continue," he commanded.

Glaring at his demanding tone, Liana raised her chin.

With a sigh of frustration, Aric combed his thick black hair back with his hand. "Please, *zjenni*. I wish only to know how my brother-at-arms fares."

"He, too, is well." Liana cocked her head as she pictured the man. "Jalen searches for someone, and the wolf Toen is with him. They follow a woman's trail along the south shore."

"A woman." Aric's voice grew hard. "Who?"

"I am unsure — but it may be Ranelle or Tierra." Liana's eyes widened as she made the mental connection. "Jalen must be going after Ranelle. I saw her in an earlier vision, racing along the sands. He's following her trail, headed in the direction of the Sorcerer's fortress!"

Aric rubbed his face with both hands, then sighed as his gaze met Liana's. "It is good. Now you need not worry for your heart-sister's wellbeing. Jalen shall rescue her more quickly than any man or being could. And with Toen's assistance, I have no doubt it will not be long before she is safe."

Relief flooded Liana. She threw her arms around Aric's neck and he stiffened. "Thank you," she whispered against his lips.

And since he made no move to kiss her, *she* kissed *him*.

Liana brushed her mouth over Aric's, tasting the breath he exhaled, wanting everything he could give her. He groaned as she traced his bottom lip with her tongue, and as his mouth opened, she pounced on the opportunity to slide into his warm recesses.

Aric all but roared, and returned her kiss, as though ravenous. Their mouths became frenzied and Liana grew dizzy, drunk with his masculine smell and intoxicated by the taste of him. Her hair caressed Aric, wrapping itself around the hands he now had buried in its strands.

The world spun around Liana, and the next thing she knew they had toppled off the log, their bodies rolling across the soft grass of the clearing. When they came to a stop, Liana found herself sitting astride Aric, her hair tangled around his wrists, binding him to her. Through his clothing she could feel his mammoth cock, and she could think of naught more than having it deep within her quim.

"*Zjenni*," Aric murmured as his mouth mated with hers. "Gods, how I want you. I have wanted you since the first moment I laid eyes upon you."

"Then take me." Liana moved her lips to his throat, tasting his salty male skin with feather strokes of her tongue. "I am yours, Aric."

"I—we cannot." Aric's voice came out in a strangled sound as her hands found the ties to his breeches. He tried to stop her from opening them, but his wrists were still bound by her tresses. "Liana. Stop. I do not wish to hurt you."

"You shan't." She all but purred as she found her prize, grasping his cock in her palm. Aric gasped as she flicked the head of his staff with her tongue. A pearl of his seed beaded at the top. "I love your taste," she murmured as she licked the semen from his cock.

"*Gods.*" Aric strained at the hair binding him, but she could tell he took care not to pull too hard, that he was afraid to hurt her.

He need not have worried, for no amount of pressure on her hair would ever harm her, although she did not feel inclined to share that information with him at the moment. She rather liked having him bound. A sort of sweet revenge for his having tied her when he took her from Fiorn.

Liana undid the rope secured around her waist and tossed it aside. The blanket slid from her body and it quickly joined the rope. She was completely naked astride Aric, her hair still binding his wrists.

"I want your cock inside of my quim," Liana demanded as moved lower on his body and slid her mouth over his staff. "Now."

"I—we—you do not understand." Aric groaned as she straightened and rubbed the soft curls of her mound, and then her wet slit against his throbbing shaft.

"I understand that I want you, and you want me." Liana leaned over him, dragging her nipples over his chest, the feel of his cock between her thighs nearly driving her mad. "Or was it a lie?"

Aric's black eyes were focused on her nipples as she rose up and brought them close to his face. "With this rigid cock between your thighs you surely feel how much I desire to be inside you. How much I want to fuck you."

Liana placed her hands on her breasts, cupping them, and then began tweaking her nipples the way she had watched Tierra touching her own in the vision. A savage growl rolled from Aric's throat, and as Liana ground her slit against his cock and pulled at her nipples, he looked as though he wanted to ravish her. She pressed herself forward so that one breast brushed his lips.

"Taste me," she begged, and at the same time allowed her tresses to release Aric's wrists.

He fisted his hands higher in her hair, forcing her down so that her nipple was fully in his mouth. Liana moaned as he suckled first one and then the other. His tongue and teeth tortured and teased her, made her so hot she thought she might burst into flame. The ache within her body grew tighter and tighter yet, and she knew she *had* to have him deep inside her.

Her knees pressed into the soft forest ground as she raised her hips and grasped Aric's cock with one hand. She placed the tip against the entrance to her quim.

"Now, Aric," she commanded. "Take me *now*."

Gods, she was killing him.

Aric grasped her slim hips in his hands, the tip of his cock already partially in Liana's quim. He trembled at the force of restraining himself from plunging into her, tearing her virgin shield.

Through the haze of his lust, a part of him knew he should stop. But as Liana sank lower on his staff, slowly taking him into her tight channel, he knew he was lost. Liana was *his* woman, and come what may, he would give his life for her.

"*Zjenni*," he groaned as he looked up into her beautiful face. "I will cause you pain."

Her tresses continued to caress him, inciting his passion even more. "You could never hurt me." Liana smiled and slowly eased herself farther down his cock, until he felt her barrier.

I want you inside me, Aric, she told him in his mind.

Aric stilled, his eyes locking with Liana's. "You spoke to me in thought."

Yes. With him partially inside her, Liana cupped her breasts while she arched her back, flicking her nipples and moaning. *Your cock feels so good. I want you to fuck me.*

He trembled violently, wanting to thrust himself deep within her. Just as he was about to gently press into her, Liana raised herself up on her knees and brought herself down hard.

She threw her head back and screamed as he ripped through her maidenhead.

And buried his cock to the hilt inside her quim.

Shocked, Aric tensed and gritted his teeth, overwhelmed with the sensation of being inside Liana. His overriding desire was to pound into her, but the thought of her being in pain held him in check. "Are you all right, my sweet one?"

Her breaths came in ragged gasps as she nodded and her gaze met his. Her sea green eyes looked glazed, yet sultry. She shifted as though becoming used to the feel of his cock inside her.

Sweat broke out on his body as she moved, and he fought against thrusting into her, fucking her like a man crazed with lust. "How does it feel?"

"Full." She wiggled and he groaned. "And perfect."

"I cannot hold back any longer, *zjenni*," he warned.

"Good." Her smile turned seductive.

Pressing her hips tight to him with his hands, Aric rolled over, causing Liana to yelp in surprise. His cock still buried inside her, Aric raised himself up on his arms and looked down at his woman.

Yes, *his* woman.

Come what may, she was his. He would go into exile for Liana and leave the kingdom to Renn, if that was what he must do.

"You are mine, Liana," he murmured as he brushed his lips over hers. "Always and forever."

Her eyes widened, and then rolled back as Aric slowly began to thrust his hips against hers, driving his cock in and out of her tight core. The need to claim her rose, filling his soul, adding fuel to his frenzy.

"Say you are mine," he demanded. "Say it!"

Liana gasped and wrapped her arms around his neck, and her hair curled around his wrists. "I am yours, Aric."

"No matter what." He stopped and stared down at her, a bead of sweat trickling down the side of his face. "Promise you will never leave me."

"I—I promise." She dug her nails into his hips. "Aric, *please.*"

He thrust into Liana. Fucked her harder and harder. Faster and faster. Tension spiraled tighter within him as he pounded into her quim.

She cried out, her body shuddering and clenching around him. A second later Aric's orgasm slammed into him, more powerful than any he had ever known. He continued moving and pulsing inside Liana until every drop of his seed had emptied into her womb.

He collapsed into Liana's arms, his sweat soaked skin pressed tight to hers.

I am yours, Liana whispered in his mind, her voice a caress and a demand all at once. *And you are mine.*

* * * * *

The following afternoon, Liana snuggled against Aric as he carried her to the Bewitching Pool. She felt sore inside and out, but content. Why hadn't he attempted to enjoy such pleasures with her before?

Aric's cock was hard once again, pressed against her hip through the fastening of his breeches. His tunic felt rough against her bare form, and she smiled. She had taken him while he was still fully clothed — all but his cock, that part of him that had given her so much pleasure.

She sighed as he nuzzled her ear while he climbed over the rise. She couldn't wait to get him naked and into the crystal waters — and then she would fuck him again.

When he reached the pool, Aric carefully stood her on the ancient steps and then began undressing. She drank her fill of his beautiful male body as she watched him shed his clothing. Powerful, clearly defined muscles. Black hair that reached his shoulders and begged for her to run her fingers through its length. Black eyes that made love to her every time he looked her way. His large cock that caused her mouth to water as she studied him. His fluid, masculine grace.

After he had tossed his clothing aside, Aric approached Liana and drew her to him, pressing his cock against her soft skin. "You take my breath away," he murmured as he kissed the corner of her mouth, then moved toward her ear. "I cannot get enough of you, sweet *zjenni*."

"I want you again." She shuddered as he traced the point of her ear with his tongue. "I love the feel of your cock moving inside me."

"Are you certain it is not too soon?" His stubble scraped the delicate skin of her neck as he eased his lips down her throat. "Surely you are too sore from the times I made love to you last night and this morning."

Liana shook her head. "I am ready for you *now*."

"Such the demanding one." Aric chuckled as his warm mouth captured her nipple, and she moaned as she thrust her hands into his silky hair. Her own tresses moved, exploring him, sliding around his shoulders as he nibbled and suckled at her breasts.

His mouth still upon her, Aric picked Liana up and carried her into the pool. She wrapped her legs around his waist and tilted her head back so that the ends of her hair dipped into the pool and grew wet, soaking up Elvin magic.

The magic seeped into her lifeforce, enhancing the erotic sensations flowing through her. She released a portion of her essence, surrounding Aric with it and allowing him to feel the intense pleasure she felt.

"Lord Ir." His voice grew hoarse and his erection enormous as he pressed her tight against him. "I have never felt such desire. Such need."

I want your cock inside me, Aric. Liana wrapped her arms around his neck and her legs around his waist. *Come inside of me.*

With a savage growl, he gripped her hips in his hands and thrust his cock inside her quim. Aric pounded into Liana, the magic of the pool enhancing the sensations of him plunging in and out. He was so big, so hard, and he filled her so deep. She couldn't imagine anything as exquisite as the feelings building up within her.

"Gods. *Ohmygods!*" She clawed at his shoulders as her orgasm burst through her body. Brilliant light exploded through her mind, flashes of color, emotion, feeling, and pleasure so intense it was almost painful.

He continued to thrust into her, drawing out the intensity of her climax. His body went taut and he bellowed as he reached his own zenith. He pulsated inside Liana, his cock throbbing so violently that aftershocks rippled throughout her body.

Aric withdrew, his staff still hard. He picked Liana up by her waist and moved to the bank, then turned her around so that her palms rested on the pool's edge. "Hold on," he commanded.

"What—" she started, and then gasped as Aric drew her thighs apart and plunged into her from behind. The sensation of him fucking her from this position was different and exciting all at once.

"I know not what you do to me, woman." He paused and caressed her buttocks, then slid his hands up to her breasts. "You are a witch. A beautiful witch-goddess."

A gasp spilled from her lips as his fingers squeezed her nipples. Slowly, then building up speed, he thrust into her while his hands played with her breasts.

Liana clung to the bank of the pool, her fingers digging into the dark soil. Her senses filled with the smells of dark loam and jensai perfume, the scent of Aric's seed mixed with the nectar between her thighs.

Aric pounded into her, his flesh slapping into hers. The only sounds she heard were the soft slosh of water as he thrust, her moans and his grunts.

Tension coiled inside Liana, and her eyes widened at the intensity of the feeling. When Aric moved one hand from her breast to her slit and the pleasure nub between her thighs, Liana screamed and buckled against the shore from the force of her orgasm.

Driving his cock into her, Aric grasped her hips, digging his fingers into her soft flesh. He shouted as he came, but did not stop thrusting until every drop of his seed was milked into her core.

Aric relaxed against Liana's back, his face buried in her hair. His cock was still inside her, his labored breathing matching hers.

"Mmmm." She sighed, enjoying the feel of him inside and out, the way her nipples pressed into the soft earth beside the pool, and the feel of the magical water surrounding them.

She couldn't imagine ever being happier.

Yet even as this thought seeped through her mind, a knot of worry began forming in her belly, although she didn't understand why. She pushed the concern aside, determined to enjoy the moment with Aric.

As they rinsed themselves clean, the Elvin magic began tugging at Liana's essence, telling her she could no longer wait to inform Aric of the rest of her vision.

I have something to tell you, she said in his mind, wanting that intimate connection with him.

Aric sighed and raked his hand through his wet hair. "I, too, have something of import to discuss."

Liana squeezed excess water from her tresses as she followed Aric out of the pool. "But first I must finish telling you of my visions."

Frowning, he turned to face her, his form magnificent in the waning afternoon light. "There was more?"

Liana resisted the urge to run her fingertips down his powerful chest, and nodded. "I saw another man." She tossed her wet hair over her shoulder and moved closer to

Aric so that she was mere inches away. "His name was Renn."

Aric drew in a deep breath and picked his breeches up from where they lay upon the shore. "My…Captain."

"Your Captain?" Liana furrowed her brow. "But—"

"Tell me what you saw," Aric said, cutting her off as he shoved his legs into his breeches and secured the ties.

Liana clenched her hands together. "In my vision I stood upon a precipice," she explained while Aric pulled his tunic over his head. Her voice wavered as she went on, and the knot in her belly grew. "A great bird approached from Mount Taka, and when it landed, it transformed into a man."

Aric stilled for a second, then grabbed his boots. "Continue."

"Your Captain is Nordain." Liana frowned as she watched Aric slide on first one boot, then the next.

"Yes." He nodded. "Did you see anything else?"

A feeling of doom gripped Liana so hard she began trembling. Something was wrong. Very wrong.

"Liana?"

She straightened and rubbed her arms from a sudden chill in her bones. Gooseflesh sprouted on her limbs and she wished she had brought the blanket to wrap around herself so that she did not feel so naked and vulnerable. "I saw the irani. Many of them."

Aric snatched up his weapon belt and strapped it on as his intense black gaze watched her.

"The Sorcerer has sent out every single irani he has in search of…" Liana's voice trailed off as Aric's dagger caught her attention. Its red stone glistened in the late afternoon sunlight like a large drop of blood.

Images flooded her mind, one after another, each one sending her reeling. The nordai at her windowsill. Black feathers on her blanket and in Aric's hair. And Renn—in her vision the stone in his dagger had matched the one in Aric's weapon.

Why he did not eat meat...because like Liana, Aric was not human. But unlike her, he was not Tanzinite.

"Oh, my gods." Liana's body shook so hard that her knees threatened to give out. Her mind could barely process the knowledge as her eyes met Aric's. Her words came out in a hoarse whisper, "You are Nordain."

"Yes." Aric's gaze held Liana's as her world came crashing down around her. "I am Aric L'tiercel, King of the Nordain."

Chapter Six

Wrapping her arms around her belly, Liana sank to the forest floor, feeling as though she might die. Blood rushed in her ears, so loud it drowned out all but the pounding of her heart and the accusations flying through her thoughts.

Gods. What have I done?

Liana stared at the ground, unable to meet Aric's gaze any longer. Her vision blurred as tears of humiliation and betrayal blinded her, and the Elves' prophecy flooded her mind.

Tanzinite woman, wingless and wan
Nordai of Power, of twins, we warn
One path to doom, enslavement and walls
With unholy mating, Dair rises or falls

She had traded her soul to not one devil, but another. She had run from the Sorcerer, only to mate with another powerful Nordain—the King himself.

And now she surely carried the fate of her world in her womb, just as the prophecy foretold. No wonder Aric hadn't revealed his identity—to gain her trust and to ensure she would receive his seed.

Yet that made no sense. If he desired this, why did he not take her when he first had the chance? Gods knew she gave him ample opportunity. *She* had seduced *him!*

Liana realized she had no one to blame but herself. Aric hadn't forced this fate upon her—she alone was responsible.

But so many would pay the consequences.

"*Zjenni.*" Aric's low voice pierced the fog of Liana's anguish.

Vaguely she realized his hands were on her shoulders, his palms hot against her bare skin. In the next moment he scooped her up, holding her tight to him in his powerful arms. As he carried her over the rise and back to the campfire, Liana began to shake uncontrollably while fighting the desire to seek solace from his warm embrace.

Aric took her to the blanket and wrapped her tight within it, as though cocooning her from the world and what she had done.

"I will rebuild the fire." Aric pressed his lips to her hair, then moved away.

When he left her huddled in the blanket, Liana felt so empty, so alone. While he stirred the coals and added kindling and dry branches, she stared into the gathering darkness. Over and over she thought, *Gods, what have I done?*

But no answer came to her silent question.

Pine logs popped and crackled in the flames as Aric strode back to Liana. She watched the sparks whirl into the darkening sky and then vanish as though they had never existed.

Perhaps it would have been better had she never existed, too.

Aric eased to the ground beside Liana, encircled her in his arms, and drew her against his chest. He murmured words in a strange tongue that somehow comforted her, even though she didn't want to be comforted—did not deserve to be comforted.

When Liana stopped shivering, Aric took her face in his hands and forced her to look at him. Her lower lip trembled and she blinked back tears as she looked at his features that had become so familiar to her, so dear to her in such a short time.

"I am sorry, *zjenni*," he whispered. His fingers were gentle as he brushed strands of her pale hair from her eyes. "The moment I snatched you from the irani's grasp, I should have told you who—and what—I am. Perhaps you would have been strong enough for the two of us." He sighed, continuing to stroke her hair. "Perhaps with your strength I would not have betrayed my people."

"What—what do you mean?" Liana put her palms on his chest, trying to push him away. But it was to no avail, as he only held her tighter. "How did you betray them?"

"The Seraphine Council sent me to prevent Zanden from claiming you." Aric moved his hands to her shoulders, his caress helping to calm her, if only a bit. "It fell upon me to prevent your union with the Sorcerer— with any Nordain male—to ensure the prophecy never comes to bear. Thus I failed my people and all of Dair."

Liana shook her head, so violently her hair fell across her face. "The fault lies entirely with me. Not with you." She squeezed her eyes tight and pressed her forehead against his strong shoulder, her tears wetting his tunic. "If I had known—"

A shuddering sigh wracked her body. Opening her eyes, she leaned back and brushed her hair out of her face as the realization came upon her. "The truth is," she said, wiping away a tear with the back of her hand, "it wouldn't have mattered if I had been aware of your identity. I wanted you so badly, I all but ignored the signs that were right before my eyes."

"I, too, believe it would have changed naught." Aric hooked a finger under Liana's chin and tipped her head back. "I have already realized that my destiny lies with you."

"But the prophecy..." Liana's stomach clenched and she fisted her hands. "And your people. I caused you to turn from your true path!"

"No, *zjenni*. Do not blame yourself." Aric kissed her brow, the feather touch of his lips causing a slight shiver to trail down her spine. "Before we mated, I had already made the decision to take you to Seraphine, the Elvin Kingdom. The wisest of their order will instruct us in what we must do."

"The Elves?" Liana studied Aric's face for a long moment. "What do you think they will say when they learn of what we have done?"

"I do not know." He shrugged and offered her a half smile. "If need be, I will gladly hand over my own kingdom to my brother Renn, and go into exile to protect my people." Aric kissed a tear from the tip of Liana's nose. "As long as you are with me, *zjenni*, my most precious, I will be able to do whatever I must."

She struggled to hold back more tears that threatened to render her speechless. She swallowed and whispered, "You would give up your family and Phoenicia...for me?"

Aric gently brushed his lips over hers. "Yes. That and more, my sweet one."

Liana threw her arms around Aric and buried her face tight against him, unable to believe she could mean that much to him. That he would go into exile — for *her*.

From the time of her first memories, she had known so little caring, so little tenderness. And no one, save her friends Ranelle and Tierra, would have made a sacrifice of any kind for her.

But this sacrifice was far too great. Liana could *not* allow Aric to give up his kingdom. She would find some way to keep the prophecy from happening, even if it meant never seeing Aric again.

The mere thought tore at Liana so badly that she began crying harder.

Never see him again? It was as though her very heart was ripped into a thousand pieces when she thought of never feeling his touch. Never seeing his smile. Never making love to him, again and again.

Gently Aric laid Liana back on the grass, forcing her to look up at him. After he unwrapped the blanket, he moved alongside her bare form. He kissed her hair, the sensation sending tremors throughout her body, and her tresses began to caress him in response. His mouth traveled to the point of her ear and he flicked his tongue against it.

"I was so frightened earlier, when you screamed in the Bewitching Pool," Aric murmured, the husky sound of his voice causing warmth to stir within her core. "I thought you were in danger, and I was scared that I might lose you." He moved his lips to her neck, raining small kisses down toward her collarbone. "I realized then that I could never bear for anything to happen to you. I would give my own life for yours."

Liana wrapped her arms around Aric's neck, and her hair caressed him as tears slid down her cheeks. "I don't know what to say."

"You need say naught." Aric rose above her, kissing her tears one-by-one. "But I shall hold you to your promise to stay with me always."

She frowned, her thoughts confused. "What promise?"

He raised one eyebrow. "The promise I demanded of you when we first mated."

"Ah." With a little smile she pulled him toward her, and kissed him softly. "You may one day regret that request."

He shook his head, his voice serious. "Never."

Aric felt such incredible warmth in his heart for Liana that he knew their mating was meant to be. It had been...*destiny*.

No matter that he had never been one to believe in such things as love and finding one's heartmate. Now he knew the truth, knew he would never let her go.

Aric began to make love to Liana, enjoying the feel of her hair snaking around his wrist and enhancing both their pleasure. He wanted to erase the doubt in her mind, and make her his in every way possible. No matter the future — they would face it together.

The salty taste of Liana's tears was on his tongue as he rained tiny kisses across her face. "I have never known such feelings," Aric whispered as he stroked his fingertips down the soft skin of her belly. "I thought only in Elvin tales did such exist."

Liana tugged at his tunic, obviously anxious to feel his skin against hers. "Did what exist?"

He helped her yank the tunic over his head and she sighed as he rubbed his naked chest against her taut nipples. "I doubted there was such a thing as a heartmate."

She paused in her attempt to get to the fastening of his breeches, and her sea green gaze met his. He smiled as she opened her mouth, then bit her lip, as though unsure of what he meant.

"What are you saying?" she finally asked.

Aric gently kissed her, then said, "I believe you are my heartmate, Liana. I know it."

A stunned expression crossed her face. "I—I..."

"Shhhh." Aric placed his fingers over her full lips. "Let me show you how I feel."

He stood and undressed as Liana watched him. Desire filled her gaze, and something more—he was sure of it. She might not realize it yet, but Aric knew that he was her heartmate just as she was his. No matter they came from opposite worlds. No matter their differences. No matter the prophecy that tried to keep them apart. They were two halves of the same stone.

Aric lowered himself between Liana's thighs and braced himself above her. He kissed her, soft and lingering, before working his way down her body, fraction by fraction. He used his lips and tongue, attempting to taste every part of her.

Firelight flickered across her pale skin as she moaned and twisted beneath his mouth and hands. When he reached the sea foam curls at the apex of her thighs, Aric stopped to scent her passion, filling his senses with the rich smell of his woman. Her jensai bloom and moonlight scent mixed with the juices of her arousal, creating a need so great that he knew he would never get enough of her.

"Please," Liana begged as she stirred restlessly. "I need you. Fuck me, Aric."

With a smile, Aric pressed his face between her thighs, causing her to cry out when he licked her clit. He grasped her ankles and placed her feet on his shoulders as he thrust two fingers inside her quim. Liana thrashed as he sucked and licked her sensitive nub, and she shrieked as she came.

She was riding out the waves of her orgasm when he reared up and slid his cock into her wet core. He bit back the primal urge to pound into her with everything he had. Instead he slowly moved in and out, intensifying the sensations she was feeling from her climax. It wasn't long before another orgasm hit her, and then another.

Aric continued to restrain himself as he made love to Liana, wanting to extend her pleasure for as long as possible. She clenched his buttocks, her fingers digging into his skin as he slowly thrust his cock in and out of her slick core while nipping at her breasts, gently flicking his tongue across each nipple.

The feelings within him strengthened as he climbed higher and higher, while he reached out to Liana with his heart, soul and with his body.

And as he achieved the pinnacle and the most magnificent orgasm he had ever known, he knew he would never let his *zjenni* go.

* * * * *

Crickets chirruped and sang in the dark forest, and frogs added their croaks to the symphony, along with the river's constant melody. Liana listened to the sounds, waiting until Aric's breathing was strong and deep.

When she was sure he was sound asleep, Liana's tresses slid across Aric's face, releasing a bit of the Elvin magic she had absorbed from the Bewitching Pool. Her lower lip trembled, but she forced herself to continue. The magical essence would ensure that she would be able to slip out of his arms without waking him, and she hoped he would continue to sleep until the morrow's first rays of sunlight.

Liana did not wish to break her promise to Aric, but it was a promise she never should have made—and wouldn't have, had she known he was the Nordain King. His people needed him, and he should not be forced to leave his kingdom for her sake. She would do what was best for him, and his people, despite the fact she would rather die than be separated from him.

Quickly she wrapped the small blanket around her body that she had used earlier as a tunic, and tied it with the rope. When she moved away from him, her stomach clenched as she took one step, and then another. She forced herself to keep going, even though she wanted to stay with Aric with all her heart and soul.

The moonlight was stronger tonight—in mere days it would be moonchange. She had to escape to the northeast, beyond Xardu Moors, beyond Wilding Wood, where Zanden's reach could not extend. If only she could fly as she had always desired to. If she had been born with wings like any other Tanzinite, she could have flown far away without a second thought.

But then if she had not been wingless, she would not have been forced to flee Zanden in the first place.

Baethel raised his head and whickered as she stole past him.

"Shhh." Liana darted a quick glance at Aric's form beside the fire, where he still lay sound asleep. "I—I need to relieve myself."

The stallion shook his big head and glanced to Aric and back to Liana.

"I will be right back," she insisted to the horse's obvious displeasure, and then slipped into the forest.

Being a Tanzinite had its advantages. Her people were cave dwellers, accustomed to seeing with little to no light. In the village she had become accustomed to the daylight, although it often bothered her eyes if the sun was too bright.

Liana's bare feet made no sound as she scurried through the dense forest. Bushes snagged at her blanket, causing it to slip below her breasts, and she felt the night's chill air hardening her nipples. She had to grasp the blanket tight to her waist with one hand as she pushed branches out of her way with the other. In her hurry she stumbled and almost fell several times as she dodged trees and boulders, and jumped over an occasional fallen log.

When she had lost her cloak in the fire, she had also lost what little wealth in *ansi* stones she'd had. But as a Seer, she hoped she would have little trouble earning enough money or food to survive.

In the lands beyond Wilding Wood she could live in obscurity to ensure the prophecy would never come to bear. A twinge of fear skittered through her at the thought of the mysteries of the wood that she would have to traverse—it was said that Faeries, dragons and other mysterious creatures dwelled within its murky depths.

Leaves and pine needles chilled her feet, and she wished she had more than the blanket for protection from the elements. But she felt guilty for taking one thing from Aric, much less any more than that. She knew how to find wild potatoes and berries for sustenance, so she would not starve. Shelter would be another matter altogether.

Baethel snorted and whickered in the distance, and Liana knew the horse was concerned that she had not returned right away. For all she knew, the beast would wake Aric at any moment. Baethel and Aric seemed to have an uncanny ability to communicate, an odd friendship of sorts.

Liana's breathing grew harsher, her lungs aching as she ran. She had to put distance between her and Aric. He would come looking for her, of that she was certain—and she did not know if she could resist him if he found her. Once she was far enough away, she would seek shelter, a location that would also serve as a suitable place to hide.

In a small clearing, a root seemed to rise up out of the darkness and caught her foot. Liana fell hard to the ground, her face buried in leaves, and pine needles poked her cheeks and her naked breasts—the scent of jensai was so strong she could scarce breathe. For a moment she simply laid still, listening for any sign that Aric was following.

She heard only the pounding of her heart and blood rushing in her ears—and then a strange buzzing. Even the crickets and owls were silent, and she no longer heard the Everlasting River's constant roar.

Strange, that.

The scent of jensai blooms was strong, too strong. Overpowering.

Liana lifted her head and her cheek brushed a soft petal before she could draw back. She rose up to her knees, and in the moonlit clearing, she found that she had fallen in a thicket of the blooms, and that it was a jensai vine she had tripped over.

A wave of dizziness swept over her and the buzzing in her ears increased — so powerful was the perfume of the jensai. She had never been so close to them before. It was forbidden for anyone but Healers to touch the blooms or the vines. Her thoughts spun and her limbs began to tremble.

When she tried to stand, Liana's legs gave out and she fell to her hands and knees. A tingling sensation erupted on her cheek where the bloom had touched. Her head swam and her sight grew dim.

Hide. She had to hide herself until the weakness passed. If it passed.

Before she could move, her tresses vibrated a warning.

Something was coming. Searching for her.

And it wasn't Aric.

The sensations multiplied, enhanced by the Elvin magic still in her tresses, and intensified by the effects of the blooms. Her throat grew dry as she tried to move on her hands and knees toward a bush. She struggled to crawl — and collapsed on her side in the middle of the jensai.

The beasts were closer now. She sensed them.

When they were almost atop her, she finally heard them through the buzz in her ears. Massive wings flapping. Pounding in her head. Slamming into her heart.

A horrible screech ripped her soul.

The clearing darkened as an enormous shadow blocked out the moonlight.

Her body went numb as she rolled onto her back. Through her blurred vision, she saw the unmistakable outline of an irani.

She had left Aric, only to fall into Zanden's hands.

Chapter Seven

Snuffling, followed by a piercing whinny, jarred Aric from his sleep. Oddly disoriented, Aric forced himself to a sitting position to find himself nose to muzzle with Baethel.

The stallion bared his teeth and whinnied again, telling Aric that Liana had fled.

Fury and the pain of her betrayal ripped through his gut — but then his Nordain warrior's senses took over.

Danger was approaching.

Still naked in his man's body, Aric snatched his abandoned clothing from the ground — and shifted into his nordai form. As always, the breeches and tunic became feathers, and his sheathed dagger was strapped to his leg.

Flapping his massive wings, Aric took to the sky. His heart pounded as his fear for Liana magnified. He sensed her terror and confusion, even before he heard the irani approach.

Aric flew toward the irani like an arrow shot from a bow. An updraft slowed his speed, but he pushed himself harder and faster. In the moonlit sky he saw the glowing red eyes of the three monsters, and he smelled their rotten meat stench.

The first beast dove into a clearing.

They had scented Liana.

With the fury of the gods, Aric soared downward, quickly closing in on the first irani. Just as the beast reached its claws to snatch Liana's still form, Aric attacked.

He drilled his hooked beak into the tender flesh at the base of the irani's neck, severing its spinal cord.

The irani somersaulted through the air and slammed headfirst into a tree. The beast fell to the ground, its body twitching and flopping. And then its glowing red eyes went black.

Aric barely had time to come out of his dive when the second irani was on his tail. The Sorcerer's filthy creature screeched as it gnashed at Aric. The irani caught one of Aric's tail feathers in its teeth and ripped it out.

Shrieking the Nordain battle cry, Aric shot forward, narrowly missing the third irani. Baethel whinnied below, and Aric glanced down just long enough to see that the stallion had arrived and now stood guard over Liana's motionless form.

Aric started to descend toward the clearing when he felt the jagged claws of an irani slash across his back. Firebolts of pain seared Aric and feathers scattered around him as he spiraled toward the ground. He struggled to pull himself to a stop, but slammed into a thick patch of grass.

Despite the pain ricocheting through him, Aric forced the change to his man's body. He ripped the dagger from its sheath and bellowed with the might of a Nordain warrior.

Weapon clenched in his hand, Aric charged the irani who now attacked Baethel. The horse whinnied and rose on his hind legs, striking out with his forelegs while protecting Liana.

With one slash of his blade, Aric beheaded the first irani he reached. Blood spurted, showering Aric, but he ignored it as he dove for the last irani. The beast's leathery wing caught Aric in the face, ripping a gash across his forehead.

Rearing back, Baethel struck the irani from the side, knocking the beast off balance. Blood poured down Aric's face as he lunged at the irani, burying his blade to the hilt in its skull. Both beast and warrior collapsed to the ground with the force of Aric's blow.

The irani continued to flap and twitch as Aric sprawled across its back. He pushed himself to a standing position and gave the dying beast one last kick to its miserable head. And then the irani lay still.

Attempting to catch his breath, Aric wiped blood from his eyes with his hand. His back and forehead burned where gashed by irani claws. Baethel whickered and stepped aside, allowing Aric to see his beautiful Liana — her face buried in jensai blooms.

"No. Gods, *no.*" Taking care not to put his own face too close to the potent blooms, Aric dove forward and scooped Liana in his arms. She was so tiny — almost weightless.

He held Liana in one arm and sprung onto Baethel's bare back. "To Seraphine," he commanded as he grabbed a fistful of Baethel's mane to steady himself. "To the Elves at once!"

Baethel bolted into the night as Aric clung to Liana, holding her small form tight to him with one arm. "*Zjenni*, what were you thinking? Why did you break your vow? Why did you attempt to leave me?"

A droplet rolled from his eye, mingling with the drying blood on his face. He scrubbed the moisture away by rubbing his cheek against his shoulder. By the gods! He was a *warrior* — King of the Nordain! He did not shed tears.

But the thought of losing his *zjenni*, his heartmate, was enough to bring him to his knees.

He would never forgive himself if Liana died.

* * * * *

A gentle caress on Liana's cheek brought her slowly out of her dream of being held by the dark stranger. She smiled as she remembered that he wasn't a stranger any longer, and that she knew him as intimately as she knew herself.

"Aric," she murmured, and her tresses moved, sliding around the hand that stroked her so gently — but when her hair touched the person it immediately stilled. It wasn't her Aric.

Liana blinked, struggling to focus on the face above her. A woman sat on the edge of the bed Liana occupied, and she had an odd glittering symbol painted onto her forehead. The woman had a smile as kind and loving as a mother for her newborn babe. Crystal blue eyes sparkled at Liana, and hair fell like the darkest honey about a face so lovely and so perfect that Liana couldn't imagine meeting anyone more beautiful.

"Who—" Liana blinked and swallowed, her throat so dry it ached. "Who are you?"

"I am Angelei." She had a musical voice that sent a small thrill throughout Liana.

Angelei lifted a golden cup to Liana's mouth, and Liana automatically parted her lips and swallowed the cool liquid. "This is *orlai*, a drink that will aid in your preparation," Angelei said as the mixture rolled over Liana's tongue. It tasted sweet. Of strawberries with a hint of wild ginger.

A warm and quite pleasant sensation spread throughout Liana's body. She felt relaxed and almost as though she'd had a bit too much ale. "Where am I?" she asked, the words feeling thick in her mouth as she spoke. "Where's Aric?"

"You are within the protective confines of Seraphine, and you will see your Aric soon." Angelei smiled and set the cup on a table beside the bed. "We brought you back to health after you nearly succumbed to the jensai. You inhaled far more of its pollen than most beings can withstand at such close proximity."

Relief flooded Liana to know that Aric was all right — and that he was there. But then she realized what else Angelei had said. "Jensai?" Liana frowned, her mind whirling from the effects of the *orlai*. "I do not remember anything beyond it being late at night..."

"Do not be concerned." The woman leaned back and tucked her dark tresses behind her delicately pointed ear, and her smile became even more radiant. "Your memories shall return."

"You are Elvin." Liana's eyes widened and warmth rushed through her as her gaze dropped from Angelei's face to her body and she realized the woman was completely naked. Angelei had a lithe body with skin the color of cream, generous breasts, and taut raspberry-colored nipples. The same glittering blue symbol that was on her forehead was also shaved into the shorn dark hair between her thighs.

When she glanced from Angelei to her own body, Liana discovered she was just as bare. Not even a blanket covered her.

"Ah..." Heat flushed Liana's face as her gaze met the Elvin woman's.

"'Tis our way." Angelei cocked her head, an amused expression on her exquisite face. "No one wears clothing within Seraphine. We believe our bodies are beautiful and that we should enjoy them—and each other's."

Angelei's gaze slid over Liana's body appreciatively. "You have a most lovely form, Tanzinite maid."

To Liana's dismay, she felt her nipples tighten and an answering tingle between her thighs down to her core. The heady effects of the drink Angelei had given Liana only seemed to magnify the sensations she was feeling. And somehow the *orlai* made her feel less embarrassed at her nakedness than she normally would.

Angelei stood in a fluid, graceful movement that reminded Liana of a cat. "Come," she said, holding her hand out to Liana. "We must prepare you to meet with the Seraphine Council."

Still flushed with a trace of self-consciousness—but mostly arousal—Liana allowed Angelei to help her to her feet. When she stood, Liana's knees threatened to buckle. In fear that she might fall, she clung to the Elvin woman's arm.

While she waited for the weakness to pass, Liana absorbed her surroundings. She was in a beautiful room that must have been a part of the forest. Walls were made of tightly woven trees and vines, laced with wildflowers in purples, pinks and yellows. The ceiling was fashioned of branches and leaves. Golden orbs hovered above, their soft light making it seem as though the room was flooded with early morning sunlight.

Much of the furniture was rich and ornate, and appeared to be carved into living trees—even the massive bed Liana had been sleeping in.

"'Tis Elvin magic that makes it appear so," Angelei said, answering Liana's unspoken thought. "We would never harm any of the goddess's living entities. She gives her gifts up to us, and we respect and care for them. They in turn care for us."

Liana smiled up at the elegant, statuesque Elvin woman. "It is all so lovely."

"The goddess blesses us." Angelei inclined her head and gestured to a doorway. "The preparations must begin."

Angelei led Liana into a hallway that was lit by the same golden globes that had been in the bedchamber. Angelei was so tall that Liana had to tilt her head back to look at the Elvin woman as they walked.

The leaves and loam made such a soft carpet beneath her feet that Liana felt as though she was walking on a cloud. And the *orlai* made her feel like her head was soaring and her skin was alive with awareness. "Where's Aric?" she asked, her body throbbing and aching for him.

The Elvin woman squeezed Liana's hand. "King Aric L'tiercel is also being prepared for the meeting. You will see him in time."

King? Liana frowned as pieces of her memory returned from that night. Aric was King...of the

Nordain...and willing to leave his people for her. And she had fled...

Liana started to ask Angelei when she would see Aric, but all she could do was gasp in amazement as the Elvin woman brought them from the hallway and outdoors to a magical place. A waterfall roared as it tumbled in silvery waves down a mountainside. At its base was a small lake of the most crystal blue — like the Bewitching Pool. Ferns, trees and flowers of every variety and color grew in abundance on the grassy shores.

Liana was in such awe that she could scarcely breathe as she was led into the lake. Unlike the Bewitching Pool, these waters felt balmy and warm as she waded into it — surely Elvin magic made it so. When the water was just below her breasts, Liana leaned back and soaked her tresses, absorbing the essence of the lake and renewing her lifeforce. Her scalp tingled and her body relaxed even more, as though the effects of the pool worked with the *orlai*.

Angelei opened a vial of cleansing gel that smelled of jasmine, and she started washing Liana's hair, just as Aric had in the Bewitching Pool.

Liana closed her eyes and leaned into Angelei's skillful hands, remembering Aric's ministrations, his touch, how he had soaped her breasts and brought her to orgasm.

She could almost *feel* it.

Her eyes flew open as she realized she *did* feel it — and gasped as she found herself looking into the emerald eyes of a musclebound brown-haired Elvin god.

"I am Tirnac." The man smiled and the symbol on his forehead glittered green as he soaped Liana's breasts. "'Tis my pleasure to assist in your preparation for the meeting."

"N—" Liana started to shake her head as Tirnac rubbed the jasmine scented gel across her nipples...and she moaned instead. She struggled against the effects of the *orlai* and her mounting arousal. "Aric...where—"

"Shhh." Angelei's fingers massaged Liana's scalp. "You are a Seer, and thus must be prepared for the Council so that your thoughts are clear and you are fully receptive to visions."

Liana caught her breath as Tirnac rubbed her belly and moved to her thighs. "I—I do not understand."

The Elvin woman soaped Liana's tresses to their ends. "Your lust for the Nordain ruler must be tempered. You cannot mate with the King again until the Council can make a determination on a course of action."

"But—" Liana gasped as Tirnac reached around to soap her buttocks, pressing his massive chest against her breasts.

The Elvin man smiled. "You will not be able to vision properly if you are not relaxed, and your desires lessened, at least temporarily."

Angelei tilted Liana's head back, rinsing the soap from her tresses, while Tirnac rinsed the soap from her body. The sensation of being washed by the two Elves—combined with the headiness of the *orlai*—was so erotic that Liana couldn't believe how incredibly aroused she was.

She wanted Aric deep within her, and she wanted him *now*.

As Angelei finished rinsing Liana's hair, she felt a warm mouth fasten on her nipple and begin suckling. At the same time Liana gasped and saw Tirnac laving at her nipple, she felt Angelei's breasts rub across her back—and then the Elvin woman slipped her hand between Liana's thighs.

"What—oh, my gods." Liana was so aroused by the experience and flushed from the *orlai,* that she could hardly think straight.

"This will help to clear your mind," Tirnac murmured as he moved to her other nipple. "Mutual pleasure between men and women is a part of the goddess's blessings."

Liana couldn't help but give herself up to the sensations. She slipped her hands into Tirnac's silky hair and held him by his pointed ears as he licked one nipple and Angelei fondled the other. He slid two long fingers inside Liana's creamy slit as Angelei stroked Liana's throbbing nub.

"You are so fair, Tanzinite maid," Tirnac murmured as he suckled her.

Angelei pressed her lips to the back of Liana's neck. "Aye, she is lovely," the Elvin woman agreed.

Tirnac's cock pressed against Liana's thigh, but he made no move to enter her. "We do not enter one who has a heartmate," Tirnac said as though he had read Liana's thoughts.

Even in her frenzied state of mind, Liana was thankful. Aric was the only man she desired to bond with in that manner. It was Aric's cock she wished was inside her right at that moment, thrusting and pounding into her.

She imagined that Tirnac's fingers were Aric's and that the mouth on her breast was his, too.

With a scream, Liana came. She would have collapsed into the pool if not for Angelei and Tirnac. They held her and stroked her hair and her body as they brought her to the shore and settled her into a cushioned chair that was so soft Liana wanted to fall asleep in it.

But when she saw Tirnac take Angelei into his arms — at the foot of the chair she was sitting in — Liana couldn't tear her eyes from them.

"You are as beautiful as the goddess," Tirnac murmured as he kissed Angelei's full lips. He moved his skillful mouth to her nipples, licking and biting them until the raspberry peaks were hard and dark red.

"Ah, Tirnac. I welcome you within," Angelei whispered, adding soft words in a foreign tongue while she stroked Tirnac's cock with her long fingers, and as she watched him suckle her. A symbol glittered in the hair around Tirnac's thick staff, matching the one on his forehead.

Liana squirmed on the chair, unable to take her eyes from the lovemaking. She couldn't believe how aroused she was as she watched the couple. She *really* wished Aric was there, and that she was taking his full, throbbing cock inside of her.

Unable to bear the incredible tension building within her, Liana spread her legs wide and eased her fingers between her thighs and stroked herself. Her wet hair caressed her shoulders as she tweaked and pinched her own nipple, her excitement mounting as the Elvin woman got down on all fours on the grass beside the lake.

Tirnac knelt behind Angelei and clenched her slender hips with his large hands. She cried out, ecstasy written across her face, as Tirnac thrust into her from behind.

The movement of Liana's hands intensified as she watched Tirnac's large cock sliding in and out of Angelei. The couple's cries of passion rose, escalating the feelings swirling inside Liana. Harder and harder Tirnac pounded into Angelei, the sound of his skin slapping hers becoming louder and louder. Angelei's breasts swayed as Tirnac filled her, and she shouted at him to thrust into her as deep as he could go.

It was too much—Liana came, her body pulsating with pleasure, and moments later Angelei and Tirnac both shouted as they climaxed.

Liana was still riding the waves of her orgasm when Tirnac knelt between her thighs and slid his fingers inside her.

"Again?" she gasped, somehow wanting more, yet wondering if she should.

"'Tis our custom," Angelei said as she settled beside Liana on the chair. "You are required to be properly prepared. Your mind must be relaxed and free to do the Council's bidding."

Before Liana could respond, the Elvin woman brought her mouth to Liana's nipple, and Tirnac buried his face between her thighs.

And then Liana was too lost in the sensations to question anything.

Hours later, when Liana had experienced more orgasms than she thought any one person could have in an entire moon cycle, she was so exhausted she was sure she could sleep for nigh on a week. But Angelei and Tirnac escorted her back to the bedchamber, and finished her preparations for the meeting. She had to admit that between the *orlai* and the orgasms she was *very* relaxed.

The Elves combed Liana's tresses until they glittered like silver moonbeams. Angelei put a circlet of gold upon Liana's brow. At the front of the circlet was a blood red stone that matched the one in Aric's dagger.

"Are you certain I cannot wear *something* when I go to this meeting?" Liana asked as Angelei rubbed a sparkling perfumed powder onto Liana's back.

Tirnac smiled and administered the powder to Liana's well suckled nipples. "'Tis not done. No one wears clothing here."

Liana caught her breath at the feeling of his palms on her sensitive breasts. "Will Aric be there?"

"Aye." Angelei placed the container of powder onto a small table. "The King is being prepared as you are."

"Prepared?" A wave of jealousy rose up in Liana, a feeling so intense that it shocked her. The thought of anyone else sucking his cock and bringing him to orgasm was too much. What if he filled an Elvin maid the way he filled her?

Liana's face burned anew as she realized she had just enjoyed climax after climax at the hands—and mouths—of these Elves.

Was Aric enjoying his preparation?

Would he feel the same overriding feelings of possessiveness at the thought of her enjoying such pleasure with anyone but him?

Chapter Eight

It took seven Elvin warriors to hold Aric to the floor, pry his jaws open and pour the *orlai* into his mouth.

"Many apologies, my Lord," Damianne said with a devious grin as she stood over him, the *enrli* symbols glittering on her forehead and in the black hair between her thighs. The nude Elvin maid's breasts swayed as she crouched and slid a tube filled with *orlai* to the back of his throat and released the liquid. "You know it must be done." She backed away when she finished giving him the dose, waiting for the potion to take effect.

The strawberry ginger taste burned Aric's throat, and he coughed as he struggled against the hands and bodies of the males holding him down. His muscles bunched with fury. *By the gods!* If he had known the Elves would insist upon the *Con'tu'a*, he would never have brought Liana here.

The ache from the gash on his forehead faded as the warm liquid flowed through his body. Aric relaxed against his will and his thoughts swam. The Elvin bastards must have given him an extra dose of the *orlai*. The naked warriors laughed as they released him, each rubbing a jaw, arm, or other body part where Aric had managed to land a blow as he attempted to fight them off.

As the warriors left the bedchamber, Kerriel, a beautiful green-eyed and golden-haired Elvin warrior, moved beside his prone position and Aric smelled her woman's juices. Her *enrli* symbol was shaved into the shorn blonde hair between her thighs and tattooed on her forehead, and like Damianne's the symbols glittered and matched the color of her eyes.

Kerriel bent and grasped Aric's hand. "Come now, you big Nordain oaf."

Damianne took his other hand and the two Elvin women helped Aric to his feet. "'Tis time for your preparations," Damianne said with laughter in her voice.

"I require no damn preparations." Aric glared at Damianne, but his words came out slurred and he stumbled into Kerriel.

The Elvin maid giggled and pressed her lithe body to his, her nipples pebble-hard against his chest. "'Tis our way, as you well know, my Lord." Kerriel stroked his thick cock that lengthened at her touch. "And your desire for the Tanzinite maid must be leashed until the Council makes its determination."

Damianne's long fingers eased through the soft hair around his bollocks. "If your lust is not reined, you might interfere with Liana's Seer's visions."

Aric shuddered with longing for his *zjenni*. It had been two days since their arrival in Seraphine. He had not been allowed to go near her, not even once, despite his rantings, ravings and threats. He needed to understand why she had tried to leave him, and then make love to her until she was senseless and neither of them could walk for a week.

"Liana," Aric mumbled in his *orlai* stupor, "I must see her."

"In good time." Damianne pulled Aric from the bedside, through a doorway, and into a bathing room. "She is being prepared as we speak."

Fury whirled within Aric and tried to rise at the thought of anyone bringing Liana to orgasm but him, however the *orlai* kept his emotions and his body in check. He knew his anger was irrational, that this was part of Elvin culture and the only way they believed a Seer could experience the purest visions. But gods knew he wanted only *his* hands on Liana's body, and not another male's.

Kerriel held tight to Aric's other arm, pushing him forward with one of her small hands to his back. The *orlai* mixture they had given him was so strong that he could barely walk, much less struggle against the women. And he wouldn't want to hurt one of them in his fit of need to get to Liana.

Steam rose from the mineral water, heated from underground hot springs. Damianne and Kerriel escorted Aric down three steps and to the edge of the bath. As he stood, the two Elvin maidens began soaping him with a sandalwood-scented potion. He flinched as Damianne washed the wound across his back, a memento of his battle with the irani. The stinging faded as Aric closed his eyes and imagined it was Liana's hands upon his chest, his buttocks...the hair around his bollocks and on his cock.

The Elves were beings of pleasure, and like the customs of his own people, it was not uncommon to share those pleasures with other than one's heartmate, except for intercourse—once a man had found his heartmate he would never enter another woman.

Yet now that he had found his own heartmate, Aric had no desire to experience any pleasure with anyone but his *zjenni*.

However, his body couldn't help but be aroused from the combination of the *orlai*, his carnal thoughts of Liana, and the naked Elvin maids caressing and stroking his body.

When he felt warmth and a sucking pressure on his cock, he opened his eyes to see Kerriel on her knees in the shallow water, taking his staff deep in her throat. "Mmmm...give me all of you, my Lord."

"You have enjoyed our ministrations many times before," Black-haired Damianne said as moved behind Kerriel, pressing her breasts against the blonde Elvin woman's back. Damianne's amethyst eyes glittered as she reached around Kerriel, fondling Kerriel's nipples with one hand and stroking between her thighs with the other. "You filled each of us with your cock several times on your last visit."

"But not now that I have found my heartmate," Aric replied through clenched teeth as Kerriel applied harder pressure on his staff.

Imagining that it was Liana who sucked his cock, Aric thrust into the Elvin maid's mouth, and then cried out as he came in her throat. Kerriel moaned with her own orgasm while she sucked down Aric's seed, and smiled as her forest green eyes met his.

Before Aric had a chance to catch his breath, Damianne traded places with Kerriel. "My turn to relieve you of your stress and taste your seed, my King," Damianne murmured. She clenched her fingers into his buttocks as she lowered her head and brought his staff to hardness once again.

Kerriel pleasured Damianne, taking her to her climax as the brunette worked her magic on Aric's cock.

As Aric came again, his thoughts were only of Liana.

* * * * *

Angelei and Tirnac escorted Liana through long winding halls lit by countless golden orbs. The *orlai* still flowed in Liana's veins, making her feel as though she was drifting down the hallway. Knowing that in moments she would stand before the Seraphine Council, her belly fluttered as though hundreds of damselflies danced within.

What would the Council determine her fate to be? And Aric's?

Would Aric be angry with her for attempting to flee when she had given him her word to stay?

Liana pressed her fist to her bare belly, as if it might stop the fluttering sensation. "Will I see Aric now?"

"Perhaps." Angelei shrugged. "It seems he was not altogether willing to participate in the preparations." She grinned over Liana's head at Tirnac. "But with a little assistance, he finally did what was required of him."

Liana frowned, uncertain as to how she should feel about those comments. Thrilled that he was unwilling? Or jealous that he had succumbed to another woman's touch?

The moment she walked into the Council Chambers, Liana felt Aric's eyes upon her. Pausing mid-step, she snapped her gaze to where he stood across the room. All of the longing filling her soul was mirrored in his black eyes, even though his expression was stern. He was so handsome standing in his naked splendor, his arms crossing his massive chest, his cock thick and full the instant their eyes met.

Liana noticed the gash across his forehead, and her Seer's instincts told her that she had been the cause.

An apology rose like a swarm of bees within her breast. *Aric, I am —*

"You cannot speak with the King." Angelei grabbed Liana's arm and tugged her toward the center of the chamber. The Elvin woman's voice had turned hard, so unlike how she had been in the bedchamber and at the lake. "Not in thought or otherwise. Keep your eyes on the Council chairs only."

Liana bit the inside of her lip, wanting to rebel as she was led toward a throne and six empty chairs arranged in a semi-circle at the front of the chamber. How had Angelei known Liana was speaking to Aric in thought? Could all Elves read her mind?

Even Liana's tresses remained still, hanging down her back and past her buttocks. She struggled to maintain her dignity although she felt as though she was on public display, completely naked for all to see. It mattered not that every other person in the room was naked as well.

Elvin men and women warriors stood guard at each of the two doors to the sides of the circular chamber. At least half a dozen warriors surrounded Aric, as though ensuring he would remain where he stood. Only Angelei and Tirnac accompanied Liana, and they left her alone and retreated once she was delivered to the center of the chamber.

Three smaller chairs on each side flanked the ornately carved throne before her. Before the throne sat an enormous golden urn, so tall that it reached Liana's waist, its top as large as a barrel of ale. Liquid glimmered at the surface of the urn, and Liana caught the unmistakable perfume of jensai blooms.

The scent brought back a rush of memories of her flight from Aric, her fall into the vines...and naught else until she woke this very morn. Her cheek tingled where it had brushed a bloom, and she raised her fingers to rub the sensation away. She felt Aric's keen gaze upon her back and she sensed the frustration roiling from him in endless waves.

A door appeared within the vine wall behind the throne. Liana's breath caught and she took a step back. Golden light outlined the male and female Council members who stepped through the doorway. Every Elvin man and woman who entered the chamber was exquisitely perfect, each more beautiful than the last.

Gracefully they each glided in to stand before a chair, and then as one they sat. Like all the other Elves Liana had seen, each had a symbol on their foreheads and below — *enrli*, Angelei had called them.

The Elvin woman who perched on the edge of the throne captured Liana's attention at once. She wore a sparkling circlet around her head and her hair hung in golden ripples over her shoulders and breasts, with only her large nipples peeking through her tresses. She had brilliant amethyst eyes, and the symbol on her forehead and between her thighs glittered purple, almost seeming to pulsate with light. She was a dazzling, ethereal being, and Liana found herself both enchanted and speechless.

I am Yanea, Queen of Seraphine, the woman spoke in Liana's thoughts. *Welcome, Tanzinite Seer Liana.*

Liana startled at the Queen's voice in her head. Never had anyone been able to speak in thought with her, and she found the experience exciting and nerve-wracking all at once.

Inclining her head in a gesture of respect, Liana said, *I thank you for your gracious hospitality, Queen Yanea.*

The Queen stood and motioned Liana to come forward and stand beside the golden urn. Yanea signaled to Angelei, who brought forth a crystal chalice. When the Queen took the goblet, Angelei bowed and retreated.

Yanea dipped the goblet into the liquid in the urn. Blood red fluid swirled within the crystal as the Queen held it out to Liana. *Drink of the Seer's potion,* she commanded. *Every last drop.*

Liana hesitated, but her instincts, along with the hardness in the Queen's amethyst eyes, made her take the goblet and put it to her lips. The bitter liquid tasted like dirt and smelled strongly of jensai. It chilled her mouth and throat as it slid past her tongue, and she began to shiver, feeling as though it iced her veins.

When Liana had emptied the chalice, her fingers were so numb she barely felt the Queen pry the container from her fingers.

Look into the sacred urn, Yanea demanded. *As you vision, I will see whatever you do.*

Liana's mind whirled as she felt Elves take her by the arms and press her toward the urn. When her hands had firmly grasped the urn's sides, Liana stared into the liquid, feeling as though she was gazing into a vat of blood. The potion sparkled and glimmered before her eyes. Liana's vision blurred and her body trembled so badly she could hardly stand.

Cold. I am so cold...

But then what she saw made her soul freeze and her core turn to ice.

Naked. Chained to an iron bed, flat on her back. The room is dark, save for moonlight pouring through the single window, and her heart beats so fast it might explode from her chest.

The moon shimmers from silver to lavender. Soon it will be moonchange, and then he will come for her.

Liana struggles against her bonds, the metal cutting into the flesh of her wrists and ankles, and she curses her weakness. Curses fate for bringing her to the Sorcerer's bed.

The moon darkens to amethyst, and she knows he's coming. Her stomach clenches and she begins to tremble as his footsteps ring in the hall like a hammer against stone. Every step closer drives the stake deeper into her heart and her destiny.

The rusty sound of a bar scraping against the door. Hinges creak and the door flings open, slamming against the stone wall. The Sorcerer strides in, naked, his cock fully erect, ready to plant his wicked seed into her womb.

His mouth slashes into a cruel grin. "Together we shall start a powerful race that will enable me to rule all of Dair." He strokes her face with his soft fingers and she recoils from his clammy touch. "This I have seen, Tanzinite maid, as have you. It is no use to fight our destiny."

Screaming, Liana fights against the chains. The Sorcerer laughs, his black eyes flashing red as he lowers himself between her thighs...

"*No!*" Liana shouted and tore herself from the vision. Shaking with icy terror, she struggled against her bonds.

I cannot get away!

"*Zjenni!*" Aric's shout pierced her confused thoughts.

"Enough," Yanea said out loud, her voice as sharp as the snap of a branch.

Liana went limp as she realized she was back in the Council Chamber. Two Elvin warriors held her hands tight to the urn. Every muscle in her body was weak with relief that she was not in the Sorcerer's bedchamber.

A vision. Only a vision.

But she almost choked on the lump that rose as she realized that her visions most often came true.

"Release me," Aric demanded from behind Liana, and she sensed him fighting his Elvin guard. He was attempting to get to her with everything he had. "Can you not see it causes her pain?"

"Silence!" The Queen turned her gaze from Liana to those gathered behind her. "The Tanzinite maid must be allowed to see what else the sacred potion can tell her."

Yanea's voice lowered as she added, "There are always two paths. Two destinies. Never one."

A smile touches Liana's lips as she rests her hand on her growing belly. Through the window of Sky Castle she sees her two-year-old twin sons at play with their Nordain cousins. Her sons are dark haired, like their father, but with pointed ears and sea green eyes like their mother.

Liana rubs her belly, wondering what her daughter will look like. Thinking of how much fun her child will have playing with her halfling and full Nordain relatives. Elvin and Nordain, Human and Nordain, Tanzinite and Nordain...Faerie and Nordain. No longer are the races segregated. They live, love and laugh together.

Hands squeeze her shoulders in a firm grip, and she looks up to see her husband. He leans down to kiss her, his lips firm yet soft against her own. "Zjenni," he murmurs.

Her heart overflows with love and contentment until she looks back out the window and sees the dark storm on the horizon...

"Zjenni," Aric murmured in Liana's thoughts, and she felt warm and secure in her dream of his love.

Faintly she heard the Queen's voice. "Leave the King be. The Tanzinite maid's visions are complete."

"My love," Aric said, and she felt lips press against her temple. "Wake. Please."

Liana blinked away the shadows and found that she was secure in Aric's arms. She looked up into his handsome face. Had he just called her his love?

"Zjenni. My most precious." He smiled and pressed kisses all over her face. "I love you so much my heart fair aches with it."

Happiness swelled within Liana, so much so she could hardly speak. "I—" Her voice creaked, as though rusty from disuse. "I—I love you, Aric."

He kissed her, long and sweet. She wrapped her arms around him, lost in the sensation of his mouth and lips on hers, the feeling of his arms around her.

"Excuse me." The Queen's voice rang out, crashing into Liana's senses. "Might we finish our proceedings?"

Heat flushed through Liana, and Aric grinned against her lips. Snickers and light laughter echoed throughout the Council chambers.

He squeezed Liana tight and helped her to stand, and she was sure she was as red as a jensai bloom from the tips of her pointed ears to her toes.

"Beg pardon, Majesty." Aric gripped Liana's hand as he bowed to the Queen. "I freely give up the Nordain Kingdom to my brother Renn, and will gladly go into exile to be with my heartmate, Liana."

"That will not be necessary." Yanea waved his words away with her slender hand, and Liana felt Aric tense beside her. "As I have long suspected, the prophecy is twofold."

Hope and concern twisted inside Liana as her visions flashed through her mind.

"Explain...if you please," Aric said, sounding as though he was clenching his teeth.

Yanea walked to her throne, sat upon it, and crossed her elegant legs at the knees. She leaned back and folded her hands in her lap. "If the Sorcerer abducts Liana and mates with her at moonchange, she will bear his children, bringing about certain doom for life as we know it."

"I will die before I allow him to touch Liana!" Aric shouted, his face red, muscles bulging with fury. "I will drive my blade through that bastard's heart."

"Allow me to finish." The Queen held up her hand. "If you, King Aric L'tiercel of Phoenicia, claim the Tanzinite maid Liana as your heartmate, 'tis possible all our futures will be very different. And for the good, I believe."

"Twins," Liana murmured as warmth filled her. "We will have twin sons."

"Sons?" Aric whispered, and Liana looked up to see his startled face.

The Queen smiled. "Liana does not yet bear your child. You must wait until moonchange to mate, and her body will take your seed."

"Moonchange?" Aric looked from the Queen to Liana and back, an unbelieving look upon his face. "She will bear my children and we shall rule together? We need not go into exile?"

"Aye." Yanea inclined her head. "As I said, you must not mate again before Moonchange. And you must keep Liana safe from the Sorcerer Zanden." The Queen's amethyst eyes darkened. "For he seeks the Tanzinite maid as we speak."

Chapter Nine

Surrounded by an Elvin guard, Aric held Liana tight in his arms as they rode Baethel toward Phoenicia the following morn. Aric reveled in the feel of her soft body and wished he could bed her at that very moment. It had been mere hours since they set out on the two-day journey. Gods knew how he would make it until moonchange.

Late morning sunlight peeked through the forest canopy, spattering the ground with light and shadow. Smells of pine and cedar met Aric's keen senses, along with the scent of rain on the horizon. Sounds of horses whickering and the clop of hooves filled the air as two dozen male and female Elvin warriors accompanied Aric and Liana on the journey to the Nordain Kingdom, the Kingdom of the Sky People.

Each warrior was clothed in full battle gear and bearing a sword along with bow and arrow, to protect the Nordain King and future Queen against the threat of the Sorcerer Zanden and his irani. Some Elves were mounted on horses, while others traveled on foot, slipping through the forest like spirits in the mist. Away from the Elvin Kingdom of Seraphine, the *enrli* symbols upon the Elves' foreheads were almost invisible to the naked eye.

So few Elvin warriors were not enough to withstand a full assault by Zanden's army, but Queen Yanea's fleetest messengers had been sent ahead to warn Renn to ready Phoenicia's warriors. The Queen had used her own Seer's powers to determine that Renn had returned to the castle—but without Jalen. Aric could have flown to

Phoenicia in no time, but he refused to leave Liana for even a moment. He would protect her from the Sorcerer with his dying breath.

Clothed in a diaphanous Elvin traveling gown in a sea green color that matched her eyes, Liana leaned back in Aric's embrace and sighed. She still wore the gold and ruby circlet around her head, and he wondered if she knew the significance of the band. He had been surprised to see it upon her when she entered the Council Chambers yesterday, and had taken it as a sign that the Elvin Council would consider his plea.

Aric was beyond grateful to the gods that he was returning to the Sky People and that he had not betrayed their trust in him. The mere thought of being disloyal to his people had been a jagged knife, twisting in his heart with every breath he took. He thanked the gods for bringing Liana into his life, and that their joining heralded new hope for their world, strengthening the bonds between all races.

But first he had to protect her against Zanden. Queen Yanea had warned that even once Aric and Liana conceived their children, the Sorcerer would be a threat until his death.

And somehow, Aric would see to it that Zanden died, whether by Aric's own hand or by the hand of one of Aric's trusted warriors.

Aric's attention came back to the soft and sensual woman in his arms as they rode Baethel. "Why did you try to leave me that night in the forest?"

Liana sighed and relaxed against him. "I did not want you to have to give up your kingdom for me." Her tresses gently stroked Aric's arm and curved around his wrist as she spoke. Her small bottom rubbed against his cock with every step the stallion made. Aric's erection grew unbearably hard, and he groaned his frustration.

"Mmmm. I feel you against me." Liana wiggled in his lap. "How much longer until moonchange?"

Aric groaned again. "Nigh on two days. And if you continue moving in such a manner, I shall spill my seed in my breeches."

Liana laughed, the sound like chimes in the breeze. "Mayhap when we stop for nourishment, I will feast on your cock. I will lick and suck you 'til your seed spills down my throat."

Lust stormed Aric's being. "You are killing me, woman." He released Baethel's reins and moved his hands to Liana's breasts and began toying with her nipples through the soft cloth.

She gasped and arched her back, pressing her breasts even harder into his palms. "The Elves…"

Aric nipped at her neck while he slid one hand into the opening of her sleeveless gown and captured her breast. "You must be taught a lesson, wench. If I could, I would fuck you on this horse, witnesses be damned."

Liana moaned and pressed tighter against his chest. "But…the Elves will see…"

"They have fallen back to allow us some privacy." Aric trailed his tongue to the point of her ear as he forced her gown up to the top of her thighs. "Though I dare say you are such a lusty wench you might enjoy being watched."

The Elves had all but vanished from sight, melding into the forest. Aric slipped his fingers into Liana's soft curls, yet did not dip them into her slit. She squirmed and moaned, but he teased her, moving his fingers across her belly, down her thighs and up, only lightly caressing where she wanted to be touched most.

"Aric...*please*," she begged. "Make me come."

"Remember when I took you from your village?" Aric trailed his lips through Liana's hair as he moved his fingers from one nipple to the other. "Your hands were bound and you laid across my lap, and at my mercy. I slid my fingers into your quim and brought you to orgasm many times."

Liana clenched her hands on Aric's thighs as she twisted in his embrace. "Stop torturing me so."

"Your naked buttocks were so beautiful in the moonlight." Aric lightly ran a finger down the slit between her thighs as he licked the bare skin at her shoulder. "How I wanted to sheath my cock in you and fuck you 'til you screamed."

"I wanted you then." Liana trembled and she placed her hand on his beneath her gown and pressed his palm between her thighs. "I wanted you the moment I first saw you in the tavern."

Aric shuddered as he thrust his fingers into Liana's quim. "When I watched you from the window, when you were pleasuring yourself, were you thinking of me?"

"*Yes*. I imagined you touching me and licking my clit." She moved her hips against his hand, rubbing hard against his cock with every movement she made. "Gods how I want you inside me. I want to fuck you *now*."

Liana's fingers dug into his thighs as he stroked her clit. "Come for me, *zjenni*," Aric murmured as he nuzzled her ear and increased the motion of his hand.

With a small cry, she reached her climax, her body pulsating with her release. Aric gritted his teeth against his own lust as he continued stroking Liana, and her body quaking as endless waves of her orgasm continued on. She begged him to stop but he was relentless until she came again. And then again.

* * * * *

Wide-awake, Liana lay between her blankets staring up at the slanted ceiling of her tent, a single candle casting shadows on the canvas walls. She folded her arms across her chest. "Damn Elves," she grumbled.

"I heard that," Damianne said as she lifted the tent flap and practically glided through the opening with Elvin grace.

Heat rose to Liana's cheeks. "I do not see why Aric and I are not allowed to be with one another at night."

The beautiful Elvin woman smiled as she knelt and began unraveling her braided black tresses. Her amethyst eyes glittered, reminding Liana of Queen Yanea. "King Aric must not spill any of his seed in your womb, and we dare not take any chances."

Liana groaned and covered her face with the light blanket, sure she was as brilliant red as one could possibly be. How could these Elves speak so easily of sex? In Fiorn only the whores and men did, but even then it was as though such pleasures were filthy, rather than as wondrous as what she had shared with Aric.

A light tug on the blanket, and Damianne pulled it away. She leaned forward so that her generous cleavage showed, her pale breasts straining against her vest, and her impish smile was mere inches from Liana. "There is naught wrong with sharing such pleasures with another woman while you wait to be with King Aric once again."

"*Damianne.*" Liana covered her burning cheeks with her hands. "It may be common amongst the Elves, but it is *not* something I am comfortable with. It would be cheating on Aric."

The Elvin woman laughed, and the symbol on her forehead glimmered. "You and the King make a fine pair indeed." Damianne moved her mouth to Liana's ear and brushed her lips against the tip. "Aye, he was fit to be tied when he was told of the preparations."

Liana shivered from the sensual contact, and then Damianne backed away. She moved to the door of the tent and looked over her shoulder, giving a wicked grin as she added, "Ah, but the King's seed tastes fine indeed."

"*What?*" Liana sat bolt upright, shouting at the closed tent flap, as Damianne had already vanished into the night. "Damn Elves!"

She grabbed the gown she had worn earlier, balled it up and threw it at the tent flap—and hit Angelei full in the face as she entered.

Angelei snapped the gown back to Liana so fast that it landed on Liana's head, covering her face. "My apologies," Liana muttered, her voice muffled as she pulled the gown off her head and then looked up into Angelei's lovely face.

"Do not let my twin's shameless humor bother you, Liana." Angelei sat cross-legged beside Liana, holding an emerald green jar and a wooden spoon in her hands.

Liana narrowed her gaze and scooted farther away on her makeshift bed. "You do not expect me to swallow any more of that or—or—lie potion."

"Nay." Angelei grinned and shook her head, her honey-brown hair falling over her shoulders, glimmering in the candlelight. "As much as I enjoyed your preparations, this is not *orlai*."

It took all Liana could not to groan in embarrassment at the memory of how wanton she had been under the influence of the *orlai*. "Well, then. What is it?"

"'Tis a gift from Tirnac and me." Angelei leaned closer and whispered, "It will allow you and King Aric to, ah, enjoy each other while you are forced to keep separate quarters."

Liana frowned. It had to be some kind of Elvin trick.

"Trust me." Angelei removed the lid from the pot and placed it on the blanket beside Liana. She dipped the spoon into the mixture and held it up to Liana's lips. "The King has already taken his dose."

"I…" Liana looked from the purple mixture on the spoon to Angelei.

Angelei gave her a solemn look. "You have my word as Yanea's daughter."

Liana's jaw dropped. "You are—"

The Elvin woman slipped the spoon into Liana's mouth so fast that she did not have time to think. She swallowed reflexively, almost choking on the thick mixture that tasted of honey and almonds. Angelei put the lid back on the jar and laughed when Liana glared at her.

Liana muttered, "That was a dirty trick."

"Aye." Angelei took the jar and spoon, slipped out the tent flap and said as she went, "But you shall thank me."

Glaring at the vacant doorway, Liana wrapped her arms around her knees and hugged herself. "Right. I will thank you, my—"

Zjenni? Aric's voice broke into her thoughts, rendering Liana speechless.

Aric, speaking to her in thought?

Liana. Close your eyes. It *was* Aric, his tone, so strong and deep that it thrilled her to her woman's core and caused her quim to dampen.

Liana lowered her eyelids—and she *saw* him in his tent. It was if she was there with him, in spirit form. He wore only his breeches and sat upon a blanket, candlelight flickering across his massive chest. His eyes were closed as he rested one arm on one upraised knee, and he raked his other hand through his thick black hair.

So much longing and desire filled Liana that it was all she could do not to scramble through the doorway of her tent, past the Elvin guard and straight into Aric's arms. *I see you, Aric. I want to touch you.*

And I see you, my beautiful zjenni. Aric sighed, passion filling his voice. *Let me view* all *of you.*

Liana gasped and opened her eyes, and her vision of Aric vanished. She shut them again and saw him, his smile devastatingly sensual.

Take off your gown, he murmured, the corner of his mouth turning up as though amused by her surprise.

Her hands trembled as she pulled at the front laces of her gown. Slowly, she let the garment slip around her shoulders, over her breasts and taught nipples to her waist.

Aric tipped his head back and groaned. *Remove it completely.*

She lightly bit her bottom lip as she stood and let the fabric drop to the floor of her tent, leaving her completely naked.

Touch your breasts, he commanded, the muscles in his biceps flexing as though he held himself back from reaching for her in his vision.

Liana eased her palms up the curve of her waist to cup her breasts. A moan escaped her lips as she lightly brushed the pads of her fingers over her nipples. *I want to see you naked*, she told him.

With his eyes still closed, Aric stood and stripped off his breeches. His cock sprung free, at its full, thick length.

I would like nothing better than to lick your body and taste the salt of your skin. Her hair caressed her naked buttocks as she plucked and tweaked her nipples, imagining Aric's hands were upon her. *I want to slide my lips over your shaft. And when you come, I will swallow every drop of your seed.*

I need you, zjenni. His groan rumbled from deep within his chest. *I want to drive my cock into your quim.*

Take yourself in hand. Liana eased her palm down her belly and into the slit below. *Let me see your pleasure.*

I can smell your rich fragrance. Aric wrapped his fingers around his cock and worked his hand from tip to base and back. *I imagine myself sliding inside your wet quim, plunging deep within you and fucking you while you scream for more.*

Yes. Liana trembled as she stroked her swollen clit with one hand and caressed one nipple with her other. *Your cock fills me, makes me feel complete.* Her belly tightened as the erotic sensations built up within her. *Harder and harder you thrust into me.*

The muscles of Aric's stomach and chest were clearly defined as his hand worked his cock. *Lord Ir, you are incredible.*

Her breathing grew shallow as she increased the intensity of her strokes. *I – I am so close. Come with me, Aric.*

Now, zjenni. Aric's muscles tensed. *Now!*

Liana cried out as her orgasm hit her, at the same moment she heard Aric's shout in her mind and saw his seed spill onto the floor of his tent. She dropped to her knees, her eyes still squeezed shut, and continued moving her fingers, her body quaking with countless aftershocks.

Ah, Liana, Aric murmured as he milked the last of his fluid from his body. *I cannot wait until we can be as one.*

* * * * *

While they rode Baethel toward Phoenicia, Liana shivered beneath Aric's cloak as a cool wind swept from the north, carrying the scent of rain. It was early evening, and soon it would be dark. She leaned back against Aric's chest, as though his warmth might ease the chill of fear that had crept into her heart.

Her tresses stirred restlessly beneath the cloak. She sensed tension within Aric, and knew he felt something amiss, too. The small group had left the D'euan Forest not long ago, and now rode upon a stretch of barren plain. They were but hours from reaching Phoenicia.

Before them a mountain rose so high its peak was shrouded in the clouds — and at its summit thrived Phoenicia, Aric's kingdom. Soon to be *their* kingdom, providing they arrived safely. Aric's brother Renn and the Nordain warriors should have been waiting for Aric's party when they left the D'euan Forest, yet there was naught but the distant rumble of thunder of the approaching storm. Elvin scouts had run ahead into the Phoenician Forest, but as of yet had not reappeared.

Once again Liana thought about the vision she'd had at the pool of Renn, and how she had thought he might be the Sorcerer. Could Aric's brother be one of the Nordain in league with Zanden?

"What is wrong?" Liana said over her shoulder to Aric, a knot of concern growing tight in her belly. "I sense something…is not quite right."

"Can you wield a weapon?" Aric's voice was almost a growl, tension roiling from him like the oncoming storm. "If need be, could you protect yourself?"

The knot inside Liana rose into her throat. "I—I have never done more than slice cheese with a knife."

"I should have prepared you." Aric slid his dagger out of its sheath and handed it by the hilt to Liana, its ruby glinting in the sunlight. "There may be naught to be concerned about, but I want you to have this. Keep it hidden within the cloak, and if man or beast comes too close, ram it into his flesh with all your might."

As she grasped the hilt, Liana trembled so badly she feared she might drop the weapon. She eased it into the folds of the cloak, her heart beating as though it would burst from her chest.

For the first time she realized the Elves were now all armed, their bows and swords at the ready and their expressions serious as their gazes roamed the sky and forest.

Liana's hair went still and her eyes widened and she sensed *his* approach. "Oh, my gods. The Sorcerer is coming!"

Chapter Ten

"Damn!" Fury burned Aric's gut as shrieks from oncoming irani rent the air.

Through a gap in the clouds, he could see the moon rising—and that it had turned the lightest shade of lavender.

Moonchange was but hours away.

By the gods.

The Sorcerer's beasts drew closer, and most surely Zanden flew with them. Aric and the Elvin warriors were still a furlong from the safety of the forest and would not have time to reach its protective confines as he had hoped. They would be forced to fight in the open, where they were most vulnerable to attack.

While withdrawing his sword from its sheath, Aric held Liana tight to him with his other arm. Lightning shattered the sky. Liana gasped as Baethel reared. Rain burst from churning black clouds and pummeled the group, soaking them in an instant.

Where the name of Dair is Renn. Where are the reinforcements?

How will I protect Liana?

Aric had no more time for thought. Countless irani and renegade Nordain, loyal to Zanden, flew at them with the speed of the storm.

"At arms," Aric commanded the Elvin warriors. He knew that every Elvin arrow would find its target, so accurate were the legendary Seraphine marksmen. It was the ground battle that would be bloody.

Aric flung back his wet hair and raised his sword, its blade glimmering in a flash of lightning as he shouted, "Hold the line... hold...hold..."

While Elvin warriors aimed their arrows at the approaching irani and traitorous Nordain, Baethel snorted and pranced. Blood charged Aric's veins and he pressed Liana's small body tighter to him. The flap of mighty wings filled the air, along with the screech of irani and roar of thunder.

Already dark skies were black with beasts when Aric shouted the command, "Fire at will!"

Elvin warriors released a flurry of arrows and reloaded so quickly their movements were but a blur. Irani and Nordain shrieked as Elvin arrows struck their marks, and wounded beings tumbled through the rain-drenched sky.

Dozens of bodies littered the ground, yet more attackers came. Nordain betrayers transformed into their man and woman forms as they landed. Shouting cries of battle and wielding daggers, they rushed the Elves and Aric on foot. Irani and more Nordain dove at Aric and the warriors from above.

Elves on horseback and on foot surrounded Aric and Liana, attempting to hold back Zanden's growing ground forces. Wielding his sword in one hand, gripping Baethel hard with his knees, Aric fought off beasts that attacked from above.

He had to protect Liana.

Smells of blood, battle and death, and the rotten meat stench of the irani, rose around them despite the pounding rain.

Through the crash of thunder and battle haze, a roar emanated from the direction of the Phoenician Forest. Aric chanced a look as he sliced his blade through an irani neck. To his immense relief, the Nordain army charged toward them through the storm, some as men and women upon horses, and others in the air in their nordai forms.

The Sorcerer comes! Liana shouted in Aric's mind. He sensed her terror as she tensed even more in his arms. *Zanden is here!*

Aric raised his sword at the same moment a Nordain dagger flipped through the air and struck Baethel in his neck.

The stallion screamed in pain and reared on his hind legs.

Liana cried out as she and Aric slid off Baethel, tumbling onto the muddy field, and the horse slammed to the ground. Battling warriors swarmed around Aric while he rolled away from the stallion's hooves and tried to shield Liana at the same time.

Aric came to his feet in a rush—

And found himself face to face with a dark-robed and foul-smelling man.

The Sorcerer. Zanden. The betraying demon himself.

His brother.

"The kingdom would have been mine had I been born but minutes before you." Zanden scowled, his face twisting in a vicious smile. "No matter, for I shall have the Tanzinite wench and we shall see who will rule all."

"Your treachery stabs my very heart." Aric gripped his sword and forced himself to face his true foe. "You despoil our lands. Murder our own people!"

Zanden shrugged. "They are naught more than a means to obtain my true destiny—as is this wench, who is *my* property."

Aric's head filled with fire. His heart blazed with rage.

Blood or no, the Sorcerer had to be stopped.

He swung his sword at the same moment a powerful blow struck his head from behind.

Blinding flashes exploded behind his eyes.

Blackness engulfed Aric...and he knew no more.

* * * * *

"Aric!" Liana screamed as his body crumpled onto the muddy battlefield. She gripped the dagger tight within the folds of her cloak. So much fury filled her at the thought of Aric dying, that for the first time in her life she wanted to *kill* someone.

The battle and storm raged as she snapped her gaze from Aric's still form to the irani that had struck Aric from behind. With a fierce cry, the Elvin warrior Angelei beheaded the beast with one stroke of her blade. She started toward Liana when an invisible force blasted her from her saddle, away from Liana and into the melee.

Liana's heart pounded as her attention riveted on the Nordain man towering over her. She had no doubt that with his sorcery, *he* had unseated Angelei. His face was dark and shadowed as in her visions, but her senses told her it could be none other than Zanden, the Nordain Sorcerer.

Something about him was familiar…yet not.

"You have led me on a fair chase, Tanzinite maid." His voice was rough and filled with a tangible evil, so powerful that it vibrated through Liana. "You will be punished when we return to my fortress."

Zanden reached his hand out in midair and made a twisting motion.

Liana cried out in shock. It had felt as though he had tweaked one of her nipples through her cloak.

He laughed. "Certainly I will enjoy your penance far more than you shall."

The coppery taste of anger and fear filled Liana's mouth. The hood of her mud and rain soaked cloak fell back, releasing her tresses as she slowly stood, still clenching the dagger's hilt in her fist.

When she fully saw his features for the first time, a cruel smile slashed the Sorcerer's face.

Liana's eyes widened. *Renn…Aric's brother?*

Zanden's smile curled into a sneer as his hand snapped out and grabbed her wrist. "No. I am not Renn, but you are correct in that I am their brother."

Before Liana had time to fully process that he had read the thought she had projected, the Sorcerer twisted her arm, forcing it behind her so that her back was pressed against him. He held his other fist beside her face and clenched it, squeezing naught but air.

Liana choked as her breathing closed off — she felt like she was being strangled, as though his long fingers grasped her throat. She had no doubt Zanden could snap her neck with a flick of his wrist. A sickeningly sweet odor swirled around her, a smell like burnt sugar.

Her eyelids fluttered as she struggled for breath, and then she realized the battle around them had stopped. During flashes of lightning she saw that a ring of Elvin warriors surrounded her and the Sorcerer—with bows drawn and arrows pointed at Zanden.

In the midst of the Elves stood an imposing Nordain warrior, his sword raised and his icy silver eyes glittering. The scar across his rugged face whitened as his features hardened.

"Think you can escape this mess, brother?" Renn shouted in a booming voice.

The invisible fingers gripping Liana's throat tightened, making it even more difficult for her to breathe, but not tight enough that she was in danger of fainting—yet. Being careful to shield her thoughts, she rotated Aric's dagger in her hand. Her hair quivered.

She would die before being taken by the Sorcerer.

Zanden raised his voice to be heard over the storm. "I can kill the Tanzinite wench in less than an instant, and be gone before you blink."

For a moment the moon appeared in a small gap in the storm clouds. Liana's heart dropped as she realized it was getting closer and closer to moonchange.

They were almost out of time.

Thunder rumbled and rain pelted Liana's face as she put her plan into action. As though caught in a gust of wind, her wet tresses snaked up the Sorcerer's arms to his shoulders.

A movement caught her eye and she saw Aric stir on the muddy ground. His gaze met hers, and she sensed at once he knew what she was about to do.

With the speed of a whirlwind, Liana's hair wrapped around Zanden's throat, choking him and severing his concentration. At the exact same moment, she raised her arm and plunged the dagger into his thigh with all her might.

Aric slammed his boot into the Sorcerer's knee.

Zanden screamed in agony as his knees buckled and he started to drop to the ground, Liana's hair still around his neck.

And then he *vanished*.

Liana's hair twisted in the wind where the Sorcerer had been, and the burnt sugar smell dissipated.

A nordai screech echoed in the storm and Liana whipped her head up to see massive black wings disappearing into swirling black clouds.

Aric surged to his feet and caught Liana to him, holding her so tight she could scarcely breathe. "*Zjenni*. By the gods, I never want to see you in such peril ever again. I was so afraid I was going to lose you."

All the emotion from the battle and Aric's obvious love for her near overwhelmed Liana. Warm tears flowed down her cheeks, mingling with the cold rain, and her voice trembled as she commanded him, "Do not ever scare me like that again, Aric of Nordain."

* * * * *

Mere hours later, as they arrived in the Nordain Kingdom, cheers rose up from the crowd that swarmed around the travelers. Countless voices urged the couple to hurry into the castle as King Aric dismounted the Elvin stallion he and Liana had borrowed. Apparently the Elves had gotten word to Aric's people, and they were prepared to accept their new Queen.

Liana's cheeks burned as embarrassment consumed her. She could not believe that everyone knew about the prophecy and that all were anxious to get her and Aric into bed together to mate before moonchange.

But at the same time, she desired him so badly she could hardly wait to get him naked and inside her.

A host of warriors had stayed behind at the battlefield to tend the wounded and the dead. Liana hoped that the casualties were few — in the rush to get the King and future Queen to Phoenicia, it had been too difficult to tell. Sorrow filled her heart for those that did not make it, and for Baethel, who had become a friend to her, as well as Aric's companion.

Accompanied by a small group of Nordain and Elvin warriors, Aric and Liana had arrived at Sky Castle in record time. During the last part of the journey from the battlefield, the storm had dissipated, allowing them to travel at a faster pace.

Liana shivered as Aric lifted her from the Elvin horse. "I can walk," she insisted, even though she loved the feel of his strong arms around her. "You're wounded."

Holding her close, Aric gave Liana a slow and sensual grin that caused her to catch her breath. "I *shall* carry *my* woman over the threshold and into my bed."

Heated desire engulfed Liana like a firestorm. To Hades with the crowd — if Aric didn't get her through that door immediately, she would take him right here and now. Modesty and inhibitions be damned.

"Well hurry, then," she demanded, and he laughed.

Within a few long strides, Aric carried her past the cheering crowd, over the threshold of Sky Castle, and into the warmth of his domain. "Welcome home, *zjenni*," he murmured in her ear as he headed straight for the winding staircase.

She was so focused on Aric that she was only vaguely aware of the beautiful realm they had entered. Rich tapestries and floor coverings, ornately carved furniture, oil paintings, vases and statues — everything passed by in a blur as Aric rushed through the common room and up the stairs.

Liana had never felt such warmth and belonging as she did in Aric's arms. She almost couldn't fathom that he was *hers*. It was as though she had conjured him up in a magical vision and she feared it all might end at any moment.

"I never realized the front door was so far from my bedchamber," Aric muttered as his boots rang against the marble floor.

"These steps would be fine," Liana teased. "You may take me right here."

"Do not tempt me, woman," he all but growled as he jogged up the endless stairs.

When they reached the landing, Aric strode through a set of open doors that led to the largest bedchamber she had ever seen. Not pausing to shut the doors behind him, Aric carried Liana straight to the massive bed that commanded the center of the candlelit room. Smells of vanilla, spices, and Aric's musky male scent filled her senses, heightening her arousal.

An enormous arched window looking out into the night sky captured her attention for one moment. The now amethyst moon was visible, shimmering high above.

It was almost moonchange.

Despite the urgent need emanating from him like lightning in a thunderstorm, Aric gently set Liana on her feet beside the bed. He quickly began stripping out of his tunic, breeches, and boots, never taking his eyes off her.

Her body vibrated with desire as she stared at Aric's gorgeous nakedness and the hunger in his eyes. Her nipples beaded into tight pearls and she ached between her thighs. She wanted to taste his skin, to swallow his seed. But more than anything she wanted his cock buried deep within her.

She let her cloak drop away, and Aric grasped the top of her gown and ripped it apart. Tossing the ruins aside, he groaned at the sight of her bare skin. In a rush he lifted her onto the bed and eased between her thighs.

"Open your eyes, *zjenni*," he commanded as she started to close them.

Her eyes widened and their gazes locked. He clasped her hands in his, and raised them over her head as he added, "I want you to see the man who loves you." And with that he slid inside her in one powerful thrust.

Liana gasped at the feel of Aric's cock as he filled her. Her tresses caressed his hands and arms. She became so lost in the sensations that her eyes started to close again.

Look at me, he demanded in her mind and her gaze riveted to his in surprise and wonder that he had been able to speak to her in thought without the Elvin potion. *Do you love me as I love you?* he asked.

She moaned and bit her lip as he rocked her body. *Gods, yes, Aric.*

Harder and faster he plunged his cock inside her, her breasts swaying with every thrust. The feel of her hands captured above her head and watching Aric as he mated with her was an incredibly erotic feeling that made her crazy with lust. Startling sensations built within, so intense she could hardly breathe.

Tell me. Aric's voice in her thoughts was a command and a loving caress all at once. *Say that you love me.*

I love you, Aric. Liana arched her back as she soared to the pinnacle. *Gods, how I love you!*

She screamed as she came, her orgasm wracking her body in wave after wave of pleasure while Aric thrust into her again and again and again.

With a shout, Aric climaxed. He continued to move inside Liana, releasing every drop of his seed into her womb.

Just as he collapsed against her, the room brightened, bathed in brilliant purple light from the open window.

Moonchange.

Aric kissed her cheek, his black eyes filled with sorrow. "I am so sorry, *zjenni*. I must go."

In a rush, he withdrew his still erect cock from inside her, bolted to his feet and swiped his clothing from the floor.

He stepped away, and in an instant transformed into an enormous black nordai.

Covering her mouth with her hands, Liana choked back a sob as Aric's wings carried him through the window and away from her.

Chapter Eleven

"Aric and the other Nordain men have been gone almost a week." Liana perched on a velvet bench in front of her mirrored dressing table, and spoke over her shoulder to Angelei. They were in the King and Queen's bedchamber, which was decorated in rich hues of royal blue, gold and cream. "Surely they should have returned by now."

"Soon," Angelei replied. In the mirror, Liana watched the Elvin woman's reflection as she stroked a jewel-encrusted hairbrush from the top of Liana's head to the end of her moonlight shaded tresses. "The men will be back when they can, and then the ceremony and feasting can begin."

As Angelei brushed Liana's hair, Liana found herself mesmerized by the naked Elvin woman's graceful movements. In the mirror she saw Angelei's high and firm breasts, her nipples large and jutting out as though she was aroused. The symbols on her forehead and in the patch of hair between her thighs glittered. Liana caught Angelei's jasmine scent, the same smell as the soap she had used to wash Liana's hair at the lake in Seraphine.

Liana swallowed as her own nipples tightened and her gaze met Angelei's in the mirror. With a sensual smile, the Elvin woman moved in front of Liana and set the brush on the dressing table. She was so close that her nipple was a hairsbreadth away from Liana.

"Your need for the King is great," Angelei murmured and stroked Liana's cheek with the back of her hand, causing gooseflesh to rise on Liana's arms. "Since Tirnac has returned to Seraphine, my needs lack fulfillment as well."

Unable to take her eyes from Angelei's crystal blue gaze, Liana nodded. "I—I can hardly wait to be with Aric."

Angelei slid her hand from Liana's cheek, along the curve of her neck and shoulder. Lightly she caressed Liana's arm through the thin material of her gown. "There is no harm, only beauty, in enjoying one another until we can once again be with our men."

Liana shivered and her eyes widened as Angelei continued, "Amongst my people our sexuality is accepted as a gift from the goddess. Even the Nordain believe such pleasures to be a part of our sensual natures. Surely you recall how much Tirnac and I enjoyed you at the lake in Seraphine?"

Liana's heart beat faster at the memory of being under the influence of the *orlai* in preparation for the Council meeting—remembering Angelei's mouth and tongue upon her breasts and between her thighs after Tirnac had brought Liana to orgasm.

Her nipples ached at the thought, and she grew wet with arousal. "I—I cannot." It was all Liana could do to refuse the Elvin woman, so inflamed were her desires. "I would feel as though I was untrue to Aric."

"I do not believe the King would mind if you experienced pleasure with another woman." Angelei smiled and picked up the sheer gown that she usually wore while walking about the castle, and slipped it over her head. The filmy material clung to her body, outlining her hard nipples, her firm breasts, slender waist and rounded buttocks.

As she glided from the King and Queen's bedchamber, Angelei said over her shoulder, "Call upon me if you change your mind."

When the door closed behind Angelei, Liana rose from the velvet bench and stood before the mirror. Thoroughly aroused, she eased the gown off her shoulders and let it drop to the floor in a silken heap.

Liana ran her hands over her breasts, down the curve of her waist to the slight flare of her hips as she studied her naked reflection. Her lips were parted, dying for Aric's kiss, or to slide down his cock. The sea foam hair at her apex was already damp, desiring him to enter her. Her nipples were hard, crying out for his mouth.

She walked across the cool stone floor of the bedchamber to the cushioned seat beneath the window that Aric had flown through almost a week ago. Her naked skin felt luxurious against the royal blue velvet as she eased onto it.

Aching with need for him, she cupped her breasts and stared out at the fleecy white clouds, searching for some sign that he was on his way back. She raised herself on her knees, her fingers rolling and pulling at her nipples, and looked down below at the expansive lawns surrounding Sky Castle.

Gods, but she needed Aric. She wanted to feel his thick shaft in her hand and suck on it. She wanted his tongue between her thighs and his cock plunging deep inside her.

Although she planned to make him pay in some creative way, she had finally forgiven him for leaving so abruptly. No matter that Aric had no control over the situation, he would have some serious penance to pay upon his return. For the gods' sakes, he should have warned her that he would have to leave as soon as it was moonchange, rather than spilling his seed and disappearing into the night.

A breeze gently blew through the window as Liana slowly ran her palms along the curve of her waist, imagining that Aric was touching her skin, his calloused fingers rough against her softness. Her hair moved down her back, caressing her buttocks, and the ache deep in her quim grew more intense.

It had taken a castle full of Nordain women, human servants, and the Elvin warriors to calm Liana and keep her from leaving Phoenicia in search of Aric so that she could give him a piece of her mind. She had known that adult Nordain males were relegated to their raven form at moonchange, but she had not realized they migrated to the northernmost reaches of the mountain during the almost weeklong event.

Still kneeling, Liana shifted on the seat so that her legs were spread apart. She slid her fingers into the patch of hair between her thighs, teasing her clit as she studied the sapphire sky in hopes she might see Aric flying home, even though it would probably not be until tomorrow. Every moonchange was different, so no one was ever sure exactly how long it would last.

Fortunately, moonchange did not affect female Nordain in the same manner as the men, so the castle and the kingdom were never left undefended. Of course the women guards outside Liana's bedchamber door, and the warriors who accompanied her everywhere, were more than an annoyance. She felt like a prisoner rather than a Queen.

And that was another thing she was going to *discuss* with Aric when she got a hold of the man, she thought as she stroked her aching bud. He had not bothered to tell her that the gold and ruby circlet upon her brow meant that she had been officially joined with him. The ceremony that his subjects were planning at this very moment was a mere formality as she was already considered to be the Queen of Phoenicia. The event would take place immediately upon the men's arrival.

Liana tipped her head back, enjoying the feel of her hair as it moved against her, and wishing it was Aric's touch. She moaned as she stroked the swollen folds of her slit and studied the sky. Clouds billowed outside the window, making her feel as though she truly was in a castle in the air.

She imagined in the future she would be looking out that very window, her hands upon the sill as Aric slid into her and fucked her from behind. It would be like making love in the clouds.

The movements of Liana's fingers intensified as she fondled her nipples with one hand and fingered herself with the other. Her hair slid across her naked back and her belly tightened. A fine sheen of perspiration coated her skin as she soared higher and higher. She pictured Aric's large cock as he thrust into her, felt him filling her aching channel, his bollocks slapping into her as he rammed her from behind and she begged him for more.

Glancing down to the expansive lawns below her window, she observed gardeners and other castle servants performing their duties in the warm morning sun. Liana was certain she could not be seen, but the thought of being watched as she pleasured herself made the sensations feel even more erotic. What would they think if they saw her caressing her own nipples and stroking her clit?

Liana's body trembled and she pumped her hips as though Aric rode her. Blood rushed in her ears and her vision blurred as she climbed higher and higher toward the peak — and then she climaxed, crying out as she came.

Her breathing was ragged as she drew out her orgasm, continuing her strokes until she could take no more.

She braced one hand against the sill to steady herself — and heard a soft moan from behind her.

Liana whirled around, almost falling off the window seat.

And saw Kerriel and Damianne in the middle of her bedchamber — naked, with Damianne suckling Kerriel's nipple.

"Beg pardon, Milady." Kerriel arched her back and gasped for breath as Damianne slid her mouth to the other nipple. "We came to see if you wished to go for a walk about the castle grounds."

Grasping the edge of the cushion to steady herself, Liana fought against waves of embarrassment at being caught pleasuring herself — and renewed desire at the sight of the Elvin women. "Wh-what are you two, ah, doing?"

Damianne sank to her knees and grasped Kerriel's hips, her mouth close to the glittering *enrli* symbol between Kerriel's shapely thighs. Damianne lowered her lids, giving Liana a sultry look as she murmured, "When we saw you reach your orgasm, we could not help but feel impassioned."

Her gaze still focused on Liana, Damianne parted Kerriel's folds and licked her with a long, slow stroke of her tongue. Kerriel cried out and slid her hands into Damianne's shimmering black hair.

Unable to move or speak, Liana's body flushed with heat and incredible desire as she watched the Elves. Gods how she wished she was with Aric right now.

Damianne paused for a moment and licked her lips as though savoring a decadent dessert. "Join us, Majesty."

"Aye," Kerriel moaned, moving her hands from Damianne's hair to caress her own breasts. "Damianne has the tongue of a goddess."

Liana's passions were at such a peak she barely had the presence of mind to shake her head in refusal. Aric had better get home *soon*, or she might just give into the carnal activities of these Elvin women.

"Then feel our pleasure if you will not join us." Damianne gave a wicked smile before continuing. Never taking her amethyst gaze from Liana, Damianne licked Kerriel in another long stroke.

Liana gasped—she *felt* Damianne's tongue when the Elvin woman lapped Kerriel. And then she felt as though hands were upon her nipples as Kerriel fondled her own breasts and watched Liana, just as Damianne was doing.

At first Liana tried to fight the sensations as Damianne licked and sucked Kerriel, but her body felt as though it was fastened to the windowsill. It was so unbelievably intense and erotic Liana could not help but become captured by the experience.

Liana's thighs widened and she braced her arms on the velvet window seat, her gaze riveted on the Elves. The scent of her own woman's passion, as well as Damianne's and Kerriel's swirled around Liana, heightening her arousal.

Kerriel began to tremble, her green eyes wide and focused on Liana. At the same moment she saw Kerriel succumb to her orgasm, Liana reached her climax. Damianne's magical tongue continued until both Liana and Kerriel begged her to stop.

"Ye, gods," Liana murmured as she melted against the velvet cushions of the window seat, feeling like she might not be able to move for at least a week. "I cannot believe that just happened."

Damianne's *enrli* symbol on her forehead sparkled as she stood, and then Kerriel lowered herself to her knees. "We are not finished yet, Majesty," Damianne said with a roguish glint in her eyes.

Before the comment had a chance to register in Liana's sated mind, Kerriel buried her face hard between Damianne's thighs and thrust three fingers into Damianne's core.

Liana's hips bucked as she cried out and held on for the ride.

Chapter Twelve

Dressed in a shimmering sleeveless gown in an effervescent sea green shade, Liana strolled through the extensive gardens of Phoenicia, trailed by her usual guard. It was the afternoon following her magical pleasuring at the hands—or rather minds—of the Elvin women. Liana had done her best to avoid Damianne and Kerriel in the hours since then, afraid of what the pair might do to her the next time they got her alone.

Liana breathed in the perfume of the garden's many flowers, but she gave the patch of jensai blooms a wide berth. The sun and all of nature filled her senses, renewing her lifeforce. Aric should arrive soon, she hoped. The Nordain women had all but promised her that moonchange had ended.

As she rounded a gurgling water fountain, Liana admired the marble sculpture at the center of the fountain. It was an erotic sculpture of a Nordain male and female, the man suckling the woman's nipples as her head was thrown back in ecstasy, and her hand grasping his enormous cock.

The sculpture made her mouth water and her body ache. She bit the inside of her lip as she turned to walk along another garden path, and almost stumbled over a pair of Nordain women in the throes of passion. Both were naked on the grass, lying in a position where each woman's face was buried between her partner's thighs. They writhed and moaned as they pleasured each other, their supple bodies gleaming in the afternoon sunlight.

Liana bit back a groan at the sight of the women who obviously could *not* wait for the men to return. It was a common occurrence around the castle, but it was about to drive her out of her mind with lust for her man.

If only Aric was with her. She would take him right there in the grass beside the women.

She shook her head at her wayward thoughts as she sought escape from the erotic scene. Casting a glance over her shoulder, she wondered if the women who were assigned as her guard were as aroused as she was after witnessing the sexual play by the fountain. The guards smiled at her, but maintained their professional demeanor. They were apparently well used to it, or at least hid their desires while performing their duties.

Now if it had been Elvin women who came upon the Nordain couple, the Elves would have joined in the pleasuring without another thought.

Liana sighed as she walked, and looked down the rolling castle grounds to where several Nordain children were at play, their mothers close by. Two boys chased one another, shrieking with laughter. The first took a running jump and transformed into a nordai, and then the second boy quickly changed and leapt into the air as well. The pair continued chasing one another in their raven forms, but stayed well in range of their mother's watchful eyes. The boys would not join the men for the moonchange migration until they reached puberty.

With a smile, Liana continued her stroll. She pressed her hand to her flat belly, still unable to believe that she was pregnant with Aric's child.

Children. We shall have twins.

It had only been a week, but there was no doubt in her mind that she carried Aric's sons, just as the vision had foretold. If it was not for her Seer's senses, then the morning sickness and the mood swings would certainly have been a sure sign. The past few days she had gone from wanting to throttle her man, to crying from missing him, to being filled with wanton desire, to dancing with joy around the castle grounds at the thought of their future children, and at the thought of the man she loved.

Whom she was going to strangle the moment she got her hands on him.

Well, after she rode him long and hard and made sure he couldn't walk for at least a fortnight. *Then* she would throttle him and make him answer all of her questions.

Including how the Sorcerer Zanden happened to be Aric's brother. And why hadn't Aric bothered to tell her? She had asked the questions of anyone who would listen, but down to the last person, they each told her it was for the King to discuss with her.

And there was something else Liana felt she needed to know. It niggled at the back of her consciousness, but she could not quite place her senses on what it was.

She drew near the castle and her thoughts turned to her friends Ranelle and Tierra, and she again wondered how they fared. On the journey from Seraphine, Aric had promised Liana that he would send out some of his finest warriors in search of Tierra. He had claimed he had no doubt that Jalen, an Elvin warrior, would easily retrieve Ranelle. Liana hoped Aric was right—she couldn't bear it if anything happened to her *halia*.

Because her visions were usually of the future, Liana didn't know if the Sorcerer had actually captured Ranelle yet, or if it was an event that might not happen if Jalen reached her first. Liana could only pray to the gods and goddesses that Jalen reached Ranelle before Zanden did.

Liana paused at a bed of roses, taking a moment to touch the petals of a deep pink bloom. The petal felt soft to the touch, reminding her of the velvety feel of the head of Aric's cock. As she stroked the petal between her thumb and forefinger, she pictured his erection in her hands when they had been at the Bewitching Pool. And then how she had slid her lips over the tip of his cock, working his shaft with her mouth, tongue and hands until he had spilled his seed into her throat —

"Your Highness." Angelei's voice crashed into Liana's erotic fantasy.

With her cheeks flaming from embarrassment, Liana straightened and faced the Elvin woman, desperately trying to think of something to say. "I—I keep telling you to call me Liana, and not Highness or Majesty."

Angelei gave her a sly smile, as though she knew what had been in Liana's thoughts. Then the Elvin woman's expression changed and her tone became serious. "You have guests waiting in the drawing room."

"Guests?" Confusion flickered through Liana. She was so far from the village she had grown up in, and her only friends were missing. "Is it Ranelle and Tierra?" she asked, a hopeful note in her voice.

Shaking her head, Angelei replied, "Nay, 'tis not the friends you have spoken of. 'Tis best you come with me. You will find out soon enough."

For a moment Liana considered trying to use her "Queen" status to demand an explanation, but she doubted it would get her anywhere. With a knot of worry in her belly and Angelei at her side, Liana headed back to the castle.

As they walked, Liana could not help but notice how transparent the Elvin woman's gown was in the sunlight, clearly showing her raspberry colored nipples and her lithe body. Liana's body had an immediate response, and she licked her lips, imagining the salty taste of Angelei's skin...

Angelei leaned close, her shoulder brushing Liana's, her voice a caress in Liana's ear. "While I am in Phoenicia, I am at your service if you wish to enjoy more Elvin pleasures."

"Ah, yes," Liana muttered, embarrassment flooding her once again that the Elvin woman had read her arousal so easily.

Liana really had to get some, and Aric damn well better get home and give it to her.

The Elvin woman gave Liana a quick grin, but as they entered the front door of the castle, Angelei's expression altered and once again she became somber. The knot of concern grew within Liana's belly as she wondered who could be waiting, and why it seemed to bother Angelei that they were here.

Angelei paused outside the drawing room door and rested her hand on Liana's shoulder. Her crystal blue eyes met Liana's. "Remember that 'tis always best to listen to all sides of a story."

"What are you talking about?" Liana narrowed her gaze. "I don't understand."

Instead of answering, Angelei gripped Liana's upper arm while opening the drawing room door, and ushered Liana inside.

Shock slammed into Liana, rendering her immobile. She barely processed Angelei's retreat as the drawing room door closing behind her.

A muscular Tanzinite man commanded the center of the drawing room. He wore a simple white cloth around his waist, his wings were folded, and his powerful arms were at his sides. Like most Tanzinites were rumored to be, the handsome man was albino. His eyes were red, his skin was even paler than Liana's, almost translucent, and his shoulder-length hair devoid of color.

Liana's heart pounded and her mouth grew dry as her attention turned to the petite woman at the man's side. The Tanzinite female's small, firm breasts were easily seen through her opaque tunic. Her wings were folded and her complexion almost as pale as the man's. But her tresses reached the back of her knees and were the same moonlight color as Liana's—and her eyes were the exact sea green shade.

The man took a step forward.

Liana stepped back.

Do not be afraid, the man said in Liana's thoughts. *I am Palme and this is Salana…we are your father and mother.*

* * * * *

Finally he was able to return to his heartmate. Aric pumped his wings harder, blood thrumming in his veins as he soared amongst the clouds and toward Sky Castle. The past week had felt like the longest moonchange of his life, passing by agonizingly slow.

The fighting drills, conditioning exercises and maneuvers he and the men had performed while in their nordai forms had done little to take his mind off Liana. More than once Renn had chastised Aric for his thoughts being elsewhere, rather than on his duties as King of the Nordain.

One day perhaps Renn would meet his own heartmate, and find his wings ruffled as well.

All Aric had been able to think of was how much he loved Liana and how badly he wanted to be with her. Every waking moment he had pictured her sweet smile, the sensuality burning in her sea green gaze, and her soft and welcoming body.

He wondered if she had pleasured herself as she thought of him, or perhaps even sampled the talents of the lusty Elvin wenches. The mere thought of his *zjenni* being pleasured by other women made his passions rise beyond belief.

Desire powered his flight as he led the flock of Nordain men back to their women. The warriors formed a V behind him, with Renn to Aric's right, and his second in command, Troyas, to his left. The morning was crisp and clean, the wind exhilarating beneath his wings.

Yet Aric's conscience bothered him. As though something was not quite right—and his *zjenni* was troubled. He had no doubt that the female warriors guarding the kingdom could fend off any invasion. They were a fine fighting force, equal to the men in intelligence and cunning, and superior in many ways.

Why then did worry gnaw at his belly?

As he spotted Sky Castle's turrets, Aric's excitement to see Liana increased, but his concern heightened as well. Could she have been injured in an accident? What of the babes she carried in her womb—were they doing well?

A furlong from the castle, Aric shrieked the traditional greeting as he passed a Nordain sentry perched on a pine. The sentry ruffled her feathers and gave Aric the all clear cry, bowing her head in respect as he flew past.

Like an arrow released from a bow, Aric shot through the air, eating up the remaining distance to the massive entrance of Sky Castle. When he was a few feet off the ground, he transformed into his nordai form, landing in a stride that carried him through the front doorway.

Behind him rang the laughter and excited cries of women greeting their men, and Aric knew the celebration was just beginning. Much mating and feasting would be occurring with the males' return, continuing well into the night, after the ceremony where Aric would publicly claim his woman.

Aric signaled to Angelei as he strode into the castle. The Elvin woman wore a clinging gown of a sheer material that displayed all of her charms to their best advantage from her dark nipples to the *enrli* symbol in the patch between her thighs. Aric decided that Liana must have a gown like it—but to wear for him only. He would not have every man ogling his wife's body.

"Where is my Queen?" Aric asked when he reached Angelei.

"My Lord." The Elvin woman bowed her head as she gestured down the hallway. "Her Majesty is with guests in the drawing room."

"Thank you, Angelei." Aric nodded as he immediately headed to Liana, his boots ringing against the stone floor. What guests could be so important that she was receiving them in the drawing room?

When he reached the room, he opened the double doors and strode through to see Liana with her back to him. She was staring at a pair of Tanzinites with an incredulous look upon her beautiful face.

"What?" Liana said, disbelief in her voice. "Who — who did you say you are?"

Aric's hackles rose at Liana's obvious distress. "Am I interrupting something?" he growled as he reached her side.

Liana whirled around, her eyes wide with relief when she realized he was there. "Aric!" she cried as she reached up and flung her arms around his neck, clinging to him as though she needed his support. "I missed you so."

"*Zjenni,*" he murmured and kissed her long and deep.

Gods but she felt soft and wonderful in his embrace, her scent of moonlight and jensai blooms enveloping him. Her taste was even sweeter than he remembered. His cock grew so rigid he feared it might burst out of his breeches. He would take her on the drawing room floor if not for the Tanzinites —

Damnation.

With reluctance Aric drew away from the kiss, and his eyes locked for a moment with Liana's. Her lips were moist and parted, her breasts rising and falling with every breath and her nipples jutting beneath the thin material of her dress. At least for the moment he had managed to take her mind off of whatever had upset her and she did not look nearly as unsettled as she had when he first walked in.

Slowly he turned away from her to the Tanzinites. "Beg pardon," Aric said as he inclined his head to the couple. "I have not seen my beautiful Queen for nigh on a week."

"Forgive our intrusion, King Aric." The Tanzinite gave a slight bow. "We well understand as we have not seen our daughter for twenty seasons."

Aric frowned. "Daughter?"

My Lord, I am Salana and this is Palme. Aric startled as the woman's gentle voice spoke in his thoughts. *We are Liana's mother and father.*

Clenching his jaw, Aric narrowed his gaze, anchored his arm around Liana's shoulders and drew her close. "You abandon your daughter as a babe, and then have the audacity to appear uninvited in my kingdom?"

Aric's protectiveness sent a swell of warmth through Liana. Never before had she felt so loved and accepted. With him at her side, she knew she could bear anything that came her way.

At Aric's harsh words, Palme raised his chin. Salana bowed her head and her wings drooped. Despite the fact that these beings had abandoned her at birth, Liana could not help but feel compassion for them.

Liana looked up at Aric and offered him a smile, telling him without words how much it meant to her that he was beside her. "Let us hear what they have to say."

His gaze met hers and he slowly nodded. "Anything for you, *zjenni*."

"You have our deepest appreciation." The Tanzinite man drew in a deep breath and he turned his red eyes from Aric to Liana. "No words exist in any language that can convey how much we grieved over losing you. Nor can they express how sorry we are that we were forced to give you up when you were born."

"Forced?" Aric's word rang out like an anvil against stone. "How could any beings be forced to give up their child, yet know that she lived in Zanden's realm and was treated as an outcast her entire life?"

"I grew up knowing only the love of my friends Ranelle and Tierra," Liana said softly. "Like me they were orphaned or discarded at birth."

The prophecy. Salana sighed, her eyes glittering as though she held back tears. *You were not discarded. The moment you were born and the Tribe saw you were without wings, you were whisked away from us.*

"Zanden was still a young Sorcerer then, as you well know." Palme's wings flexed as he spoke, as though stirring with anger. "He swore he would have Liana killed if we did not leave her to live in Fiorn until her twentieth season."

Aric stiffened beside Liana at the mention of the Sorcerer. His arm tightened around her shoulders, and she felt tension radiating from him.

We could not bear for anything to happen to you. Salana's sea green eyes pleaded for forgiveness, her voice soft and sweet in Liana's thoughts. *The Tanzinite people have not the means to protect themselves from the Sorcerer.*

"Thus we waited and hoped that the dual prophecy would turn for the good of us all." Palme folded his arms across his chest. And then his voice lowered and Liana felt the caring in his words. "Especially for you, Liana. Although you never saw us, we ensured your safety and wellbeing throughout your years in Fiorn."

"What do you want from her now?" Aric demanded before Liana could respond.

"We want nothing for ourselves." Palme's gaze met Liana's and his stern features relaxed into a semblance of a smile. "It pleases us greatly that you are now safe from Zanden and happy with your new husband. Truly our only desire is that you know you have always been loved. We would have given anything to change the past."

You are our only child. Tears flowed freely down Salana's pale face. *We hope you can find it in your heart to forgive us.*

Throughout the exchange, Liana had been overcome by a sense of the surreal, and felt almost numb. But as she listened to Salana's and Palme's story, and sensed kindness and love radiating from them, tremendous warmth filled her.

With a smile to Aric, Liana tore herself from his grasp and went to her birth parents. "When I was a little girl, I oft dreamed that you would come to me and say these very words."

She fell into Salana's embrace, and tears coursed Liana's cheeks, mingling with her birth mother's. Their essences mingled, and Salana's hair caressed Liana's shoulder. Liana felt a kinship with her mother that she had never felt with anyone else.

I would be pleased to have the opportunity to know you and become friends, Liana told Salana as she pulled away, projecting her thoughts to Aric and Palme as well.

"Yes." Aric's expression relaxed as he stepped forward to shake hands with Palme and then kissed the back of Salana's hand. "We would be honored to have you as our guests at our joining celebration."

Chapter Thirteen

An hour later, Liana was clothed in a ceremonial gown that glittered with thousands of diamonds scattered across the silvery dark material. Angelei was brushing Liana's tresses, making her hair shimmer down the back of her gown like moonlight against a star spattered sky.

In moments Liana would be going to the Grand Hall to be officially joined with Aric in the eyes of his people. Elvin, Nordain, and Human royalty would be in attendance, along with Liana's birth parents.

If only Ranelle and Tierra could be with Liana now, the day would be perfect.

She pressed her hand against the flutter in her belly as she stood before the mirror in her bedchamber, waiting for Angelei to finish fussing with her tresses. The diaphanous gown Liana wore had been a gift from the Elvin women — Liana thought it beautiful, although she was nervous at how revealing it was.

The front of the bodice was a mere two strips of gathered material from shoulders to waist, not quite enough to completely cover each of her breasts. The train of her gown was as long as the length of Liana's bedchamber; however, the material at the front of the skirt was gathered up to the apex of her thighs, completely exposing her legs and barley covering her woman's curls.

Angelei slid the gold and ruby circlet upon Liana's brow, stepped back and smiled. "Come, 'tis time."

Liana's lips trembled as she attempted her own smile. "Thank you," she murmured as she reached up to touch the circlet with her fingertips.

Heat rose in Liana's cheeks as they walked past the mirror and she saw how much of her pale breasts showed beneath the silvery strips of fabric. The gown shifted over her breasts, her nipples jutting out prominently.

Ye gods. One wrong move and she would spill out of the gown, allowing the guests to see more of their Queen than she would like them to.

Angelei and Liana left the bedchamber and were met by Kerriel and Damianne on the landing. "You are truly a beautiful Queen, Milady," Angelei said.

"I'm going to be an exposed Queen if I'm not careful," Liana muttered and the Elvin women laughed.

Earlier, Liana and Aric had been forcefully separated the moment they left their Tanzinite guests in the drawing room. Giggling with fiendish delight, the Elvin women had swarmed around Liana and had taken her from Aric in order to prepare for the joining celebration.

But my gods, she had wanted to have her own *private* joining with Aric *before* the celebration.

Nordain men, including Renn, had been on hand to thwart Aric's attempts to remain with Liana, and to ensure he would be readied for the celebration as well. From the men's remarks, Liana had a feeling that Aric's preparation involved a great deal of ale and male bonding.

Surely he would rather have been bonding with her.

While damselflies invaded Liana's belly, the Elvin women escorted her from the bedchamber to the Grand Hall. When Liana and her attendants reached the closed doors of the Hall, Liana stopped to take a deep breath and shore up her courage.

Kerriel stood before the doors, prepared to open them at Liana's command. Like the other Elvin women, Kerriel was clothed in a transparent thigh-length gown that clearly showed her lovely form, from her dark nipples to the *enrli* symbol between her thighs. No doubt after this celebration countless more ballads would be written about the sultry and sensual Elves.

"So fair you are, Queen Liana." Kerriel tucked a strand of her golden hair behind her pointed ear and smiled. "You and the King shall make a most beautiful joining."

"Aye, Milady," Damianne agreed with a sly grin. "If you wish to broaden your pleasures in your marriage bed, Angelei, Kerriel and I would be delighted to join you and the King this eve."

"I think not." Liana groaned and rolled her eyes to the ornate ceiling. "You are all too much."

"Or perhaps just right?" Angelei teased and pressed her soft lips to Liana's ear, causing Liana to shiver. "May the blessings of the goddess be with you and King Aric during this joining celebration, and for all eternity."

* * * * *

Aric clenched his hands as he stood alone before the dais and ceremonial table at the head of the Grand Hall, waiting for Liana's entrance. Behind the table was an enormous carved throne cushioned in deep red velvet. Nordain delicacies were arranged upon the surface of the ceremonial table, all surrounding a single gold chalice with a blood red ruby in the middle of the stem.

At each corner of the head of the room were large pots of living jensai, lending the Hall with their sweet perfume. The sacred vines were in full bloom—*the same shade of rose as Liana's delightful nipples*, Aric thought with a lust-filled sigh.

Thanks to his brother Renn and Nordain warriors plying him with ale, Aric was more relaxed than he otherwise would have been as he waited for Liana—yet he still managed to feel restless and edgy.

What was taking his Queen so long?

Countless guests filled the massive Hall, seated at dozens of tables lining both sides of an isle that ran the length of the long room. The Hall buzzed with laughter and conversation, along with the clink of glasses and sounds of chairs scraping against the stone floor.

Every table was set with fine linens, sparkling crystal goblets, glittering silver plates, and bottles of the finest Elvin wines. Delicious aromas filled the room: roasted, steamed, and fresh vegetables, fruits of every variety, baked breads and rolls, pastries and sugar seed cakes, and myriads of other gourmet dishes.

Roses of every color from the royal gardens lined the isle Liana would walk upon as she came to him. Huge bouquets of pink roses occupied the center of every table.

Someone clapped Aric's shoulder, startling him from his thoughts. Aric turned and saw that it was his brother.

"What would you like as your joining gift, brother?" Renn asked.

"Joining gift, eh?" Aric frowned as he considered Renn's question. "It would please my Queen if you would seek out her friend, Tierra. The maid lived in Fiorn with

Liana, but my *zjenni* believes Tierra has vanished from the village."

Renn cocked an eyebrow. "A vision?"

With a nod, Aric replied, "Yes. And I fear my sweet Queen will not rest until Tierra is found."

"Consider it done. For our Queen and my future nephews." Renn bowed moved to a nearby table to sample a seedcake from a tray.

Aric turned his gaze to the rich tapestries that hung along the walls. Each panel depicted a scene from Nordain life and customs. Among Aric's personal favorites was a tapestry showing a couple making love in their human forms; as well as the one next to it that depicted the same couple enjoying sex as nordai, their wings spread wide and the male impaling the female from behind.

Aric groaned as his cock throbbed to mate with Liana. It had been a week—far too long. He would not be able to experience a true nordai mating with his *zjenni*, but truly only Liana mattered to him. When they were joined, he planned to keep her in their bedchamber for twice the length of time he had been kept from her.

At least.

To Hades with the ceremony—he had waited long enough. He would track Liana down and claim her in his own fashion.

As Aric started to step forward, the double doors at the opposite end of the hall opened, and he stopped in his tracks.

Damianne and Kerriel glided in, and then stood to each side of the doors. Aric almost smiled at the sound of nearly every male in the room sucking in his breath at the sight of the nearly naked Elvin women.

But then Liana walked through the entrance and Aric's heart nearly ceased to beat.

Gods, but she was lovely. From across the Hall her sea green gaze met his, and it was all he could do to rein himself in. He couldn't take his eyes from her and the sparkling gown she wore — if one could call it that — that barely hid her nipples. And if it had been cut any higher in the front, she would be showing her sea foam curls to every man in the room.

As Liana slowly walked toward him, Aric swallowed. Hard. His throat grew dry as he vacillated between wanting to take her right here in the Hall, guests be damned — or cover her, hiding her near nakedness so that no other man could look upon her beautiful body but him.

He was leaning rather heavily toward taking her right here and now.

Angelei trailed Liana, holding up the end of the long train. Aric was profoundly pleased that following Liana there was an almost naked Elvin woman for the men to stare at, rather than his Queen.

Liana's radiant smile grew brighter yet when she reached him. As she finally stood at his side, Angelei arranged the train at Liana's feet and then stepped to the guest table to the right of the ceremonial dais.

"*Zjenni*, my Queen," Aric murmured as he took both her hands in his and kissed the back of each one. "Gods, but I am the most fortunate of men."

"As I am the most blessed of all women, my King." Liana reached up to kiss him and he almost stopped breathing when her gown pulled against her breasts and he saw the edge of her rosy areola.

Her lips met his and applause broke out in the Hall.

Lord Ir, but he had forgotten anyone existed but the sensuous woman before him.

Aric lifted his head and smiled when he saw Liana blushing a pretty pink from the tips of her pointed ears down every part of her exposed flesh.

Clasping one of Liana's hands and raising it between them, Aric turned to the guests and bowed, as did Liana, whose breasts moved dangerously closer to freeing themselves from their scanty bonds. The room burst into another round of applause, and did not quiet until Aric held up his free hand.

"I present to you my wife, Queen Liana," Aric's voice boomed through the now silent room. He looked down at his woman and smiled. "My *zjenni*, my heartmate."

When Aric's gaze met Liana's, her heart filled near to bursting with love for him. The way he looked at her, the intensity in his black eyes, made her feel as though she was the most beautiful and most loved woman on all of Dair.

More applause thundered through the Hall until Queen Yanea of the Elvin Kingdom of Seraphine rose from the guest table to the right of the dais. Liana caught her breath at the sight of the ethereal woman, and sensed that everyone else in the room had done the same.

Not even a whisper broke the silence as the golden-haired Elvin goddess glided across the floor toward Aric and Liana. She wore a sheer gown, clearly showing her large nipples and generous breasts, her dress similar to the Elvin women who had attended Liana.

The amethyst-eyed Queen's *enrli* symbol glittered upon her forehead and between her thighs as she came to a stand before the ceremonial table. She wrapped her elegant fingers around the stem of the ruby and gold goblet, and brought it before the Nordain King and Queen.

Yanea inclined her head first to Aric and then Liana. "I am honored that you have asked that I assist in your joining."

He bowed and replied, "The honor is ours, Queen Yanea."

Liana's heart beat faster as she wondered what was in the goblet, and prayed it was not the erotic *orlai* or the Seer's potion. Gods only knew what she might be forced to do in front of all of these people if it was either of those fluids. And what of the babes she carried?

The elixir will not enter your womb, Yanea reassured Liana in thought. *Your sons will be fine, as will you. This is neither orlai nor Seer's potion.*

With a smile, Yanea lifted the chalice to Aric's lips. "Drink of the Nordain joining elixir and share with your mate."

Aric sipped from the elixir, then bent down to Liana and placed his mouth to hers. She closed her eyes and parted her lips to welcome his kiss, but to her surprise, he slowly released the fluid into her mouth from his—like a raven feeding his mate.

Liana's mind whirled as she accepted the elixir from Aric. She grasped his powerful arms, digging her nails into his biceps and clinging to him for fear she might fall from the intense sensations. Heady warmth filled Liana as the raspberry taste flowed over her tongue, and her hair tingled from her scalp to the end of her sensitive tresses. Her desire for him soared, her abdomen tightening. Her nipples swelled and hardened, and she grew incredibly wet for him between her thighs.

Aric finished feeding her the liquid, but then pressed his muscled body tight to hers, deepening the moment with a kiss that inflamed her senses even more. She felt his stone-hard cock against her belly and sensed the fierce desire emanating from him.

When he withdrew from the kiss, Liana opened her eyes to see that Aric's were heavy lidded. His hands gripped her shoulders as though he feared losing control of his passion. Liana could think of nothing but how much she wanted her husband to let loose his desire and how she wanted him deep within her.

Yanea's clear voice interrupted Liana's thoughts, jarring her back to the present. "'Tis your turn, Queen Liana."

Intoxicated from the small amount of elixir, Liana's belly fluttered at the thought of doing the same to her husband. Carefully she drank from the cup when Yanea lifted it to her lips, and then held the elixir in her mouth.

Aric bent down as Liana reached up to meet him. When their lips touched, she opened her mouth and he gently sucked the fluid from her until it was gone and he had swallowed every drop.

In the next instant, Aric vibrated with lust. His cock ached and throbbed to be buried in his *zjenni*, and his muscles trembled with the force of his desire. He wrapped his huge hands around Liana's tiny waist and picked her up, molding her soft body against him as he claimed her mouth. She clung to him and returned the kiss, matching all the passion in his soul.

Applause erupted in the room.

Aric and Liana stilled.

"I keep forgetting we are not alone," he muttered as he lowered her back to the floor.

"Are we finished?" Liana whispered in his ear before he straightened. "May we go to our bedchamber now? I need you so badly I can hardly stand it."

"Ah, my sweet *zjenni*." Aric groaned, barely able to pull himself away from her. "The ceremony has only just begun."

The look of intense disappointment on Liana's face made him smile, and he brushed his fingertips along her jaw. He clasped her hand and turned to the crowded room. "Let the joining celebration begin!" he shouted.

The crowd roared and the guests began eating the first course spread out upon the tables.

Aric swung Liana up into his arms and she squealed with surprise, wrapping her arms around his neck as though she feared he might drop her. He carried her around the ceremonial table to the throne where he seated himself with Liana in his lap. The joining elixir thrummed through his veins, and he had to struggle not to feel and taste her right here in the Great Hall.

She tried to sit up, her breast straining against the thin strips of cloth covering her nipples, but he held her so that she was partially reclining. "Aric! I cannot spend the entire ceremony like this."

He brushed his lips across hers as he settled one hand high on the inside of her exposed thigh. "This is part of the joining. If we do not carry out the tradition, my people will not allow us to leave the room."

Before she could protest further, Damianne and Kerriel approached, each with a black silk cloth in their hands.

Liana's jaw dropped as she looked from the Elvin women to Aric. "You're not going to tie me up, are you?"

With a grin, Aric replied, "Not exactly."

Kerriel secured a cloth around Aric's eyes, and then Damianne tied a matching black band around Liana's. The Elvin woman brushed her hard nipples against Liana's back and whispered, "Enjoy the joining feast, Milady."

With the heady feeling from the elixir still running through Liana, the feel of Damianne's breasts stimulated Liana's already lust-ridden body and she almost moaned out loud.

She could *not* believe she was sitting in front of a roomful of people and was expected to eat her joining feast *blindfolded*. But the experience heightened her senses more than she could have imagined. Her tresses vibrated and slid over Aric's arms, and she felt his hard arousal against her buttocks. His hand was hot on the inside of her thigh, mere inches from the center that ached for him.

Her essence soaked in the feel of the air, drinking in the smells and sounds in the hall. Laughter and comments floated up to her from the guests as they enjoyed their meals, along with the sounds of silverware clattering against plates and glasses clinking as toasts were made. The smells of roasted vegetables, pastries and desserts filled her nose and made her mouth water.

Aric's lips met her forehead, and as he rained kisses all over her face, he murmured, "In a darkened room filled with a thousand people, I would find you, *zjenni*."

She opened her mouth to respond, but he slipped something hard and sweet between her lips—and then it began melting upon her tongue. It was nothing like she had ever tasted before. She savored the sensation and all but moaned, "Mmmmm."

"*Chocolatyl*, a treat made of a rare plant from a country to the south," Aric said as he slipped another piece into her mouth. "It is known to be an aphrodisiac." He pressed his lips against hers and he dipped his tongue inside, sharing the *chocolatyl* with her.

Liana shivered, and she almost whimpered when he drew away. He placed a piece of fruit in her mouth and as she bit into it, juices from the raspberry squirted upon her tongue. Aric again tasted the food from her mouth. The feeling of sharing her food with Aric in such a manner was completely erotic and intoxicating.

Aric fed her a tangy piece of cheese next, and as he savored it with her, he slid his hand further up the inside of her thigh, close to her weeping core.

Gods, how she wanted him to touch her there.

But Aric, we are in front of hundreds of people, she said to him in thought.

"Do not worry," he murmured as he removed his mouth from hers. "We are alone behind the table, and no one can see what I might do with my hands."

Liana opened her mouth to protest, but Aric pushed another piece of fruit between her lips, and she bit into it. *Strawberry.*

Again he tasted the fruit from her mouth, but at the same time he began lightly running his fingers through her woman's curls.

He swallowed her gasp as he deepened the touch, slipping his fingers between her folds, and his other hand upon her near-naked breast. The elixir still ran rampant throughout, and the combination of it and what Aric was doing to her body was too much. She became so lost in the feel of his hands that she was barely aware of the sounds of people enjoying the celebration. Being blindfolded, it was almost as though they were alone in the room.

Aric's motions intensified as he slid his fingers deep into her quim, and then rubbed her oversensitive clit, his kiss deep and passionate. Tighter and tighter the feelings wound inside Liana until her orgasm exploded through her body. If not for Aric's mouth against hers, she would have screamed with the force of her climax.

Aric held her close as her body shuddered and trembled. "I love you, *zjenni*," he whispered.

In the next instant he stood and she grasped him around the neck, hanging on as her world spun behind her blindfold. As he held Liana cradled in his arms, Aric shouted, "Consider us joined."

Amid thunderous applause, Aric strode out the Great Hall, carrying Liana to their bedchamber.

Chapter Fourteen

Holding his *zjenni* close, Aric strode down the length of the Great Hall. Angelei followed, carrying the end of the train to Liana's gown. He could barely rein in his urge to rush from the hall to reach their bedchamber as quickly as possible.

"You may remove the blindfold now," he murmured to Liana as he walked through the crowded Hall.

She bit her lip. "I am far too embarrassed after what we just did. I'm not sure I want to see anyone's face just yet."

Aric laughed and kissed each of her eyes through the silken blindfold.

The applause continued as he passed visiting royalty from other kingdoms. Liana's Tanzinite birth parents smiled proudly, and he saw Salana's eyes glittering with tears.

When he finally reached the double doors, Troyas, his second in command, slapped Aric on the back. "Enjoy the rest of the ceremony with your lovely bride," he said with a wink. Troyas ogled the near-naked Elvin woman carrying Liana's train and gave a lusty sigh.

Renn stood at the entrance with his arms folded across his chest, and shook his head. "You shall never see me behave like a sotted fool over a pretty little wench."

"The wench you speak of is my Queen and yours," Aric returned with a grin. "And one day you will choke on those words, my brother."

Renn merely grunted as Aric left the Hall with Liana, Angelei in their wake.

They reached the bedchamber and Aric strode through the double doors and stopped in the middle of the floor. Angelei unfastened the train from the back of Liana's dress and took it into the wardrobe.

When Aric lowered the still blindfolded Liana to her feet, the movement caused her breasts to spring free of the thin straps.

Raw need slammed into him when he saw her bare nipples and he swooped down to capture the hard bud between his teeth.

Liana moaned as she arched her back and pressed herself into his mouth.

"Pardon?" Angelei's clear voice broke into Aric's fierce claiming of his woman.

Liana gasped and pulled off the blindfold, and Aric lifted his head to see Angelei mere inches from them.

"I have a joining gift for you both from Yanea." Angelei curtsied and held out her hand. A small crystal bottle, no bigger than a strawberry, sat in the middle of her palm. "'Tis for Queen Liana, so that she might experience a true Nordain mating on this eve."

Still holding onto Liana with one arm, Aric took the vial from Angelei, his puzzled gaze focused on her crystal blue eyes. As it dawned on him exactly what the Elvin woman meant, he smiled and inclined his head. "It is a rare gift she bestows upon us. Please give Yanea our deepest gratitude."

"Aye, my Lord." Angelei bowed and exited the room, closing the doors behind her as she went.

"What is it?" Liana quirked her brow as she glanced from the crystal bottle to Aric. "I cannot say I completely trust those Elves."

"Do you trust me?" Aric withdrew the stopper from the bottle and raised it to Liana's lips.

"With my life," she whispered and drank the potion.

It tasted like the *chocolatyl* — sweet and thick and rich. Liana closed her eyes as she savored the taste. "I feel wonderfully light. As though I am naught more than air."

"Open your eyes and imagine you are a raven," Aric whispered, his voice as smooth and intoxicating as the potion. "Feel your body find its new form as you take flight as a nordai."

Liana lifted her lids, and when she glanced down she saw sparkles — small flashes of light — all around her. Her heart pounded as she realized she was actually transforming into a nordai.

Queen Yanea had truly given her an incredible gift. A Tanzinite born without wings, destined never to fly — until this very moment.

"Take flight!" Aric said as she transformed — her gown becoming feathers as her body became fully nordai.

In the next instant, Liana spread her wings. Her raven's feet lifted from the floor, and she was *flying.*

She laughed out loud, the sound coming out like a raven's cry as she soared around the bedchamber and toward the window. Aric stood there grinning, and then he shifted to his nordai form and followed her out the arched window and into the twilight.

Gods but the feeling of the wind in her wings and Aric at her side was incredible. They flew over the castle, glided above the gardens and then over the Everlasting

River as the sunset cast rainbows through its churning waters. Screeching and calling as nordai, Aric and Liana floated on the wind and soared through the clouds.

When Liana was ready for a rest, she swooped down to the garden and settled on the statue of the mating Nordain male and female. Aric landed beside her and nuzzled her feathers with his beak.

I love you so, Liana told him in thought.

And I love you, zjenni, he responded, and Liana realized the Queen had given them yet another gift for their joining eve, allowing them to communicate in thought. *I want to mate with you as nordai*, Aric continued, his desire clearly spilling into her thoughts.

Liana ruffled her feathers. *Gods, yes.*

Aric fluttered his massive wings until he was above her — and then he entered her from behind, filling her as only he could.

* * * * *

Their desires raging even more after their nordai joining, Aric and Liana rushed back to the castle. They soared through their bedroom window, wingtip to wingtip. At least a dozen candles of plum and spices had been lit in their absence, filling the room with their warm scent and a celestial glow.

The moment Aric transformed into his human male form, his cock went rigid with lust for his *zjenni*. His blood raged as he watched his Queen return to her woman's form, wearing the revealing ceremonial gown.

They stood before the window seat. Liana was a hairsbreadth from him, her cheeks flushed, her breasts free of their bonds. The front of her gown was slightly skewed, almost revealing her soft mound.

He knew he should go slowly on their joining night, but he could not wait another moment to enter her.

Aric pulled her roughly against him and rubbed his hard cock against her belly. "I need you, Liana," he rumbled as he lowered his head and suckled one of her nipples.

"Now, Aric," she commanded, her voice hoarse with passion. "Fuck me now!"

He moved Liana to the window seat, waiting only long enough to unfasten his breeches and free his cock. She braced her arms on the window seat and spread her thighs wide. In one powerful thrust, Aric entered Liana's slick channel.

Liana cried out as she looked down and watched his long, hard cock plunge in and out of her. Aric hooked his arms under her knees as he slammed into Liana, harder and deeper. Fast and furious he ground into her soft mound.

"More," Liana begged. "Give me all of your cock!"

Aric felt Liana tense as she reached the brink of her orgasm. She bucked her hips and screamed as she climaxed, sending Aric spiraling over the pinnacle with her. His cock pulsed and throbbed within her core, shooting his semen into her womb.

Sated for the moment, Liana sprawled on the window seat with her gown around her waist and Aric between her thighs. His muscled body was heavy but comfortable as he relaxed against her, their breathing in sync with one another. Their bodies were slick with sweat, the smell of their sex warm and erotic.

That feeling niggled at her again, that there was something she needed to know, yet she couldn't quite place her senses on it.

Aric stirred, his cock still embedded deep within her, and Liana tipped her head back and moaned. His hands braced to either side of her, he murmured, "You are an incredible woman, my Queen."

Almost of its own accord, Liana felt her hand drawn to Aric's temple. "I—I..."

The moment her palm touched his forehead, everything around her vanished and blurred as she fell into a vision.

Liana blinked, trying to discern her surroundings. She was in a dark room with only the light of the moon spilling through the window to see by.

A movement caught her eye. Her heart pounded as she watched a man slither from the shadows like a wraith. Something about him was familiar, as though she had seen him before.

He reached into a cradle and picked up a sleeping child. Silently he stole from the room, and as he carried the tiny girl, Liana realized they were in a castle.

Sky Castle.

The room dissolved and Liana found herself in Fiorn, standing before the cottage where she spent her childhood. The same man from the castle appeared from the darkness, carrying the toddler to the cottage. An old woman came to the door and took the child from his arms.

The blanket fell away to reveal the dark haired girl who opened her eyes.

Silver eyes.

Oh my gods.

Liana's glazed vision slowly came back into focus and she realized she was back in the bedchamber with Aric. He was on his knees between her thighs, holding her hands in his and murmuring her name, calling her from her trance.

"Do you have a sister?" she asked, her voice hoarse as her gaze met his.

Aric stilled and then nodded. "Carilee. The night our parents were murdered, Carilee vanished. She was but a toddler, and my brothers and I were young men. We spent months doing all we could in our attempt to find her, but feared her long dead."

Taking a deep breath, Liana swallowed the lump in her throat. "Your sister is alive. She is — my *halia*, my friend Ranelle."

For a moment Aric could not process what Liana had said. Ranelle. Her friend.

The *gishla?*

Suddenly everything made sense. His wanting to cover the *gishla's* naked body whenever he saw her, and his desire to help her during the fire when he had forced himself to focus only on Liana's rescue.

Liana cupped his face, her palms soft against the stubble on his cheeks. Her lips trembled as she forced a smile. "Jalen will bring her back. For both of us."

Still crouched between Liana's thighs, Aric put his hands on the window seat and fought for control. "Zanden," he growled. "He has her and would not know she is our sister. What if he forces her to —" Aric could not utter the despicable thought aloud.

Liana closed her eyes for a moment and then opened them to meet Aric's gaze. "He knows. He is the one who stole her from the castle."

"*What?*" Aric pushed away from Liana and stood, pulling his breeches back up as he moved. Memory after memory of the time before Carilee's disappearance scrolled through his mind as he tried to make sense of it all.

"It was he," Liana said, her voice certain.

"No. He was as distraught as we were." He raked both hands through his hair, desiring to yank it out in frustration. "It was months after her disappearance when he turned traitor and became apprentice to Sorcerer Voral. Before he murdered Voral and took his place as Lord of Voral's realm."

The pieces began falling into place in his mind and he buried his face in his hands. "Lord Ir. All along it was our brother, and we never realized the extent of his treachery."

"Jalen will find her," Liana whispered, and then Aric felt her soft body press against his, and she slid her arms around his waist in a fierce hug.

Aric lowered his hands from his face and embraced her tightly to him, never wanting to let her go. While he held Liana, her moonlight tresses caressed his arms, and he felt stronger from her love. Together they would face anything that came their way.

For a long time they held each other, and Liana felt warm and loved. Fear also for her friend, but hope at the same time.

With a deep sigh, Aric lifted Liana, cradling her in his arms. "Thank you, my love," he murmured. "You are truly a gift of the gods."

"As are you." Liana slid her hands around his neck and moved her mouth to her husband's cheek. His stubble felt rough against her lips as she rained soft kisses on his chin, his nose and his eyes.

Almost reverently he carried her to the bed and laid her upon it. While their eyes were focused on one another, Aric eased the straps of her gown from her shoulders, the light touch of his calloused fingertips sending shivers of desires through Liana. She knew that she would never get enough of this man. *Her* man.

He lowered his head and kissed her soft skin as he removed her gown. His lips moved from her neck to her collarbone, and brushed over each bare nipple. Gently he eased the gown further down over her hips, and trailed his lips through her soft woman's curls, and then flicked his tongue once over her clit.

Heat filled Liana, and she whimpered beneath his sensual touch. So slowly he continued removing her gown, kissing the insides of her thighs, and her knees. As he finally slid the gown completely off and tossed it aside. She trembled as he kissed each of her feet and stroked his tongue along each bare toe.

Never taking his eyes from hers, Aric backed away, toeing off his boots. When he began unlacing his tunic, Liana stopped him. "My turn," she murmured.

A rumble emanated from his chest as she eased off the bed and came to him. She pushed his tunic up and pressed her lips against his hard abdomen. Liana started her own slow and sensuous assault, kissing his chest and licking his hardened nipples.

As Aric pulled his tunic over his head, Liana went for his breeches. Her lips roamed the flat of his stomach and lower, enjoying the taste of his salty skin, his male scent filling her senses. She tugged his breeches over his hips and moved her mouth over the cloud of soft hair surrounding his cock and stroked the sack beneath, enjoying the feel of his bollocks in her palm.

While pushing his breeches past his knees and to the floor, Liana brushed her lips along his thick cock. He sucked in his breath as she flicked out her tongue and tasted the pearl of his seed at the velvety soft tip.

In a rush Aric stepped out of his breeches, swept Liana into his arms, and carried her back to the bed. The covers felt like silk against her back as she spread her thighs and her arms, welcoming her man.

He raised her legs so that her ankles were around his neck, and then he slid into her in one powerful thrust. Liana gasped at the sensation of him filling her so deeply. For a moment he waited, just looking at her.

Candlelight flickered over their bodies, reminding Liana of the first night she had pleasured herself, and Aric had watched her from the window in his nordai form.

In long, slow thrusts, he began to move his cock in and out of her wet quim—his gaze never left hers as he moved within her. The feel of him so deep inside her was intense as Liana clenched her hands on his thighs, her ankles still high and around his neck.

"More," Liana begged. "Give me every bit of you."

"You have all of me," Aric murmured. "I am yours, *zjenni.*"

He clenched his jaw as he made love to her, his strokes becoming harder and more powerful. "Yes," she cried, digging her nails into his thighs, every muscle in her body tightening. "I love you, Aric. Come with me!"

Aric's body corded at the same moment Liana reached her climax and screamed his name. He shouted as he spilled his seed into her womb, his cry mingling with hers.

Their thoughts blended together as they spiraled down from the pinnacle, their bodies locked together, still fused as one.

Glossary

Ansi — gems used for barter

Angelei — Elvin princess and warrior; Damianne's twin and Jalen's sister

Aric — King of the Nordain

Baethel — Aric's stallion

Bewitching Pool — magical pool in the D'euan Forest

Con'tu'a — erotic Elvin ceremony designed to clear a Seer's mind

D'euan Forest — where the Bewitching Pool is

Dair — their continent

Damianne — Elvin princess and warrior; Angelei's twin and Jalen's sister

Elves — tall, sensual, beautiful beings.

Enrli — Symbol of significance to the Seraphine Elves

Everlasting River — in the D'euan Forest

Faeries — mischievous and erotic beings who reside in Wilding Wood

Fiorn — the village in Zanden's realm where Liana was raised

Gishla — exotic dancer

Halia — heart-sister

Ir — god of the Nordain

Irani — winged beasts of the Sorcerer

Jalen—Aric's Elvin brother-at-arms; brother to twins Angelei and Damianne

Jensai—sacred vines with heavily scented blooms

Kerriel—Female Elvin warrior

Liana—Tanzinite female banished at birth to live with humans because she was born without wings

About the author:

Cheyenne is a thirty-something wild thing at heart, with a passion for sensual romance and a happily-ever-after...but always with a twist. A University of Arizona alumnus, Chey has been writing ever since she can remember, back to her kindergarten days when she penned her first poem. She always knew that one day she would write novels, and with her love of fantasy and romance, combined with her passionate nature, Romantica is a perfect genre for her.

In addition to her adult work, Chey is also published in young adult literary fiction under another name. Chey enjoys spending time with her husband and three sons, traveling, working out at the health club, playing racquetball, and of course writing, writing, writing.

Cheyenne McCray welcomes mail from readers. You can write to her c/o Ellora's Cave Publishing at P.O. Box 787, Hudson, Ohio 44236-0787.

Also by CHEYENNE MCCRAY:

- Seraphine Chronicles 2: Bewitched
- Seraphine Chronicles 3: Spellbound
- Seraphine Chronicles 4: Untamed
- Wildfire
- Wildcat
- Wildcard

Why an electronic book?

We live in the Information Age — an exciting time in the history of human civilization in which technology rules supreme and continues to progress in leaps and bounds every minute of every hour of every day. For a multitude of reasons, more and more avid literary fans are opting to purchase e-books instead of paperbacks. The question to those not yet initiated to the world of electronic reading is simply: *why?*

1. *Price.* An electronic title at Ellora's Cave Publishing runs anywhere from 40-75% less than the cover price of the <u>exact same title</u> in paperback format. Why? Cold mathematics. It is less expensive to publish an e-book than it is to publish a paperback, so the savings are passed along to the consumer.

2. *Space.* Running out of room to house your paperback books? That is one worry you will never have with electronic novels. For a low one-time cost, you can purchase a handheld computer designed specifically for e-reading purposes. Many e-readers are larger than the average handheld, giving you plenty of screen room. Better yet, hundreds of titles can be stored within your new library — a single microchip. (Please note that Ellora's Cave does not endorse any specific brands. You can check our website at www.ellorascave.com for customer recommendations we make available to new consumers.)

3. *Mobility.* Because your new library now consists of only a microchip, your entire cache of books can be taken with you wherever you go.

4. *Personal preferences are accounted for.* Are the words you are currently reading too small? Too large? Too... **ANNOYING**? Paperback books cannot be modified according to personal preferences, but e-books can.

5. *Innovation.* The way you read a book is not the only advancement the Information Age has gifted the literary community with. There is also the factor of what you can read. Ellora's Cave Publishing will be introducing a new line of interactive titles that are available in e-book format only.

6. *Instant gratification.* Is it the middle of the night and all the bookstores are closed? Are you tired of waiting days — sometimes weeks — for online and offline bookstores to ship the novels you bought? Ellora's Cave Publishing sells instantaneous downloads 24 hours a day, 7 days a week, 365 days a year. Our e-book delivery system is 100% automated, meaning your order is filled as soon as you pay for it.

Those are a few of the top reasons why electronic novels are displacing paperbacks for many an avid reader. As always, Ellora's Cave Publishing welcomes your questions and comments. We invite you to email us at service@ellorascave.com or write to us directly at: P.O. Box 787, Hudson, Ohio 44236-0787.

Printed in the United States
24636LVS00004BA/169-408